RETRO VERSION

MISSION 6 OF THE BLACK OCEAN SERIES

J. S. MORIN

Retro Version

Mission 6 of: Black Ocean

Magical Scrivener Press 22 Hawkstead Hollow Nashua, NH 03063

www.magicalscrivener.com

Publisher's Note: This is a work of fiction. Names, characters, places, and incidents are a product of the author's imagination. Locales and public names are sometimes used for atmospheric purposes. Any resemblance to actual people, living or dead, or to businesses, companies, events, institutions, or locales is completely coincidental.

Ordering Information: Special discounts are available on quantity purchases by corporations, associations, and others. For details, contact the publisher at the address above.

J.S. Morin — First Edition

ISBN: 978-1-939233-74-5

Printed in the United States of America

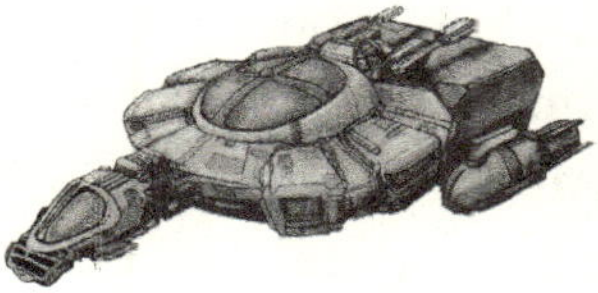

RETRO VERSION

It was a somber duty to inform someone of her brother's death, but it was bizarre to instead notify her that it was all faked. Tanny closed the taxi door, and the petrol-burning relic grumbled and rolled away. She was left standing on asphalt black-top that wound its way through rows of tiny wooden houses, each fenced in by white pickets surrounding bright green patches of lawn. The smell of petrol exhaust mixed with fresh-cut grass and grilled meat from a barbecue taking place down the street.

Checking her datapad to verify that she had the right address, Tanny hopped the low picket fence of 413 Mapleview Terrace and strode up to the front door. The only hint of a control console or door alarm was a single plain button set into a wrought iron fixture. Pressing it caused a two-tone bell to ring inside the residence. Tanny stood at military ease and waited.

Hard-shod footsteps approached from inside. A moment later the door opened. "Hi, Tanny. Funny seeing you here," Rhiannon Ramsey said. She wore a floral top with slim slacks and low-heeled shoes. Her bouffant hair was bleached blonde and locked in place with hairspray. Every bit of her looked completely adapted to the retrovert surroundings. Carl's parents' predilection for the middle twentieth century had seeped into her to the bone. But through the veneer of her retrovert trappings, Tanny could see the tension in her shoulders and neck, the quiver in her lip.

"Rhiannon Ramsey," Tanny said, her tone clipped and military. "I regret to inform you that your older brother, Bradley Carlin Ramsey, is alive and well and every bit the asshole he's always been."

Rhiannon breathed a sigh and a weary smile crossed her face. "Come on in. I just made lemonade."

Tanny stepped past as Rhiannon held the screen door. It swung closed behind her, pulled by a spring. "Sorry if he worried you. We couldn't risk broadcasting, since this place has no security encryption."

Rhiannon led the way through a tiny family room and into the kitchen. The lone table was circular and less than a meter in diameter, flanked by a pair of wooden chairs. Rhiannon poured two glasses of the promised lemonade from a glass pitcher with lemon slices and ice cubes floating at the top. "You park the *Mobius* anywhere around here? How's Mort?"

"No, we're at the spaceport," Tanny replied, accepting a glass. She winced at the overpowering sourness as she took an experimental sip. "You're taking this a lot better than I'd expected."

Rhiannon sighed. "Who in the galaxy has a brother who says to wait three months after word comes that he's dead?"

"You knew?" Tanny said. She blinked to make sure she was seeing Carl's little sister, the reluctant retrovert, and not some ARGO special agent. "He didn't even tell *us* until the last minute."

"Typical," Rhiannon muttered. "No, but he clued me in years ago that something like this might go down. It's our old man's rule, really. Carl just tuned in, and I tuned out. He stole the Squall, right?"

Tanny took a long swallow of lemonade. It was refreshing once she got over the sourness. "You sure you're in the right line of work?"

"Singing's a lot safer than the shit my brother gets himself into," Rhiannon replied. "But it makes sense. That whole racing crash while he was out of scanner view was just too fucking convenient. So either he'd died doing something stupid —which is my guess as to how he *will* die one of these days—or he was playing an angle."

"But what makes you think he could have snuck a Squall out from under everyone's noses?"

Rhiannon smirked. "C'mon, Tanny. I flew with Mort as long as Carl did, back when he the old man ran together."

Tanny glanced into the adjacent bedroom and washroom. The bedsheets were rumpled, thrown into the middle from two sides. Towels littered the floor beside the shower. "Where's Derek?"

Rhiannon rolled her eyes. "Get it together; you're three boyfriends behind. Me and Derek split after the show on Paris VII. Lloyd's down at the golf course with his buddies."

"What's he do?" Tanny asked. Rhiannon was too much like her brother, sometimes.

"Golfs, mostly," Rhiannon said. "But when he does work, he's a TV producer. On-world stuff. Between you and me, mostly shit. We don't even watch the boob tube though; we've got a holovid in the basement."

Tanny bit back a snide comment. Wouldn't Rhiannon ever quit chasing show-biz types? "Living the life, huh?"

"Hey, I don't mind the style, but this place takes it a *little* too far sometimes," Rhiannon said. "Living here's good for my career, but I won't retire here. Hell, even the 'rents couldn't put up with this place forever."

"Any chance we can find someplace local to crash until things blow over?" Tanny asked.

"We've got a spare bedroom, but not enough for your whole crew. Besides, I'm guessing my brother's gotta lay low. You're welcome to stay though. I can never get a straight story from him about what he does between visits."

"Sure," Tanny replied. "I'll just let them know."

"Roddy can blend in," Rhiannon said. "It's not remotely authentic, but the laaku population's going up every year. I think it's close to 15% by now. Mort and Chip can obviously—"

"Chip's dead," Tanny said, feeling the familiar knot twist in her stomach. She hadn't thought about Chip in weeks. "Salvage accident."

Rhiannon had her arms around Tanny in an instant. "No way! I'm so sorry."

Tanny let herself be comforted for the sudden pang she felt. They had been close once, briefly. Each was as close to a sister as the other had ever known. "It's all right. He went quickly, at least." In her heels, Rhiannon was the taller of the two of them. Tanny rested her head on her ex-sister-in-law's shoulder and felt tears well in her eyes. It must have been something in the Ramsey blood that knew how to cut through the leather around her heart. "It was my fault. I promised my aunt and uncle I'd look after him."

Esper looked over her shoulder as the shuttle-port disappeared behind a bend in the forest path. Gravel crunched beneath her boots, stiff knee-highs still too new to be comfortable. It felt as if she were walking into another world, which was silly because that was *exactly* what she was doing. Except that this world wasn't from her time, or even Mort's for that matter.

"You'll trip on your own feet if you don't mind where you're going," Mort admonished her. He was dressed in his formal robes and fit into the setting better than she would have expected. The staff he used for a walking stick looked less like a prop than it normally did aboard the *Mobius*.

"I just feel like we ought to be doing more than waiting," Esper replied. "Kubu's out there with that crazy laaku woman, and we're visiting a medieval colony."

"Where we'll meet with the woman who's going to help us get him back," Mort said. "This isn't a time for rashness or impatience. Who'd have imagined a wizardess would go to the trouble and paperwork to officially adopt him?"

"Sneaking in, grabbing him, and running away seems like a perfectly viable option," Esper said. "You said yourself that laaku aren't very good wizards."

Mort sighed and looked up into the trees, ignoring his own advice to watch his footing. The forest trail was well worn, but unpaved and not very level. It wound and twisted, with the occasional tree root poking up to hook unwary toes. Birdsong filled the air, along with the scent of evergreen. "I could do just that, you know—lead a magical assault and get Kubu back in one piece. Probably."

"Then why don't we?" Esper asked. She hurried ahead two paces and turned to face Mort, blocking his way. "When did we become so cautious? Just because Kubu isn't human?"

Mort stopped. "I have been on the run for twenty years—at least for some loose definition of running. I have been hounded, pursued, ambushed, and assaulted. Reward-seekers have tried to poison me, slit my throat in my sleep, and lure me aboard a ship with the life-support system rigged to explode. These incidents have come fewer and farther between over the years, but when I hear that one of our friends has been kidnapped by a wizard—laaku or not—it raises my hackles."

Esper swallowed. Mort had never told her much about the Convocations attempts to apprehend him. "I'm sorry. I just assumed—"

"By all accounts, he's being treated well. Were it otherwise, I would throw myself beneath the headsman's axe to rescue him. But I haven't lived all this while with a price on my head by acting rashly. We'll meet my contact at a little place I bought years ago, when I had more optimism than financial sense. It's as secure a spot as we're likely to find."

Esper frowned at him, but Mort smirked in reply. "How far is it to this place of yours?" she asked, resuming her walk. Much as she had grown accustomed to her utilitarian shipboard garb, it was nice to feel the swish of a dress at her legs again. She looked every bit the medieval noblewoman—minus a fortune in jewelry.

Mort fell into step beside her. "Far enough. But there's a stable not far from here. We'll ride from there."

"Ride?" Esper asked. "You didn't tell me I'd be riding. I'm not dressed for it. You could have mentioned something at the shops." The gift shop at the starport had authentic attire for any of the individual colonies on Peractorum. Mort had declared his Convocation getup to be more than sufficient, but he'd watched her pick out her own outfit without saying a word about needing to be fit for horseback.

"You know how to ride a horse?" Mort asked skeptically.

"Yes. Well, sort of. I took lessons, but I quit after just a couple. I didn't like how sore I got after. Point is, I've sat on a moving horse before, and I was *not* wearing a dress for it."

"Well, the good news is that's not the sort of riding I had in mind," Mort said, waggling his eyebrows. Esper shrank back in disgust at his insinuation before realizing that his double-entendre was more likely a triple-entendre—and she had fallen for it.

"That's not nice, you know," she scolded him.

"You're the nice one," Mort replied. "I'm the dark sorcerer, remember? Speaking of which, around here I go by another name."

"Of course you do..."

"Can't very well own property when I'm supposedly a fugitive."

"Don't see how you could."

"So if anyone asks, I'm Mordred Pendergast," Mort replied. "You can still call me Mort."

"Mordred?" Esper echoed. "Like the Mordred from King Arthur? Isn't that a bit heavy handed?"

"A bit stuffy, perhaps, but our kind get away with a lot of that," Mort said. "And around here? Even if it's taken for an alias, it's perfectly in-character for the locale."

Esper looked off into the trees and let a quiet sigh of exasperation escape her lips.

"Don't you roll your eyes at me," Mort scolded. Esper shot him a glare. "Your eyes *exude* rolling. I don't need to see them. Doesn't take magic, either. Aha, there. Up ahead, there are the stables."

The forest gave way to a knot of buildings too few to be called a hamlet. They all wore thatched roofs as if in costume for the period. Their walls were daub and wattle, and their windows were simple cutouts devoid of glass. A pair of droop-jowled hounds bounded down the lone dirt road to greet them. They circled Mort and Esper, sniffing as their tails wagged frantically.

A sharp whistle pierced the breezy air. "Peotan, Geslit, leave them be," a stable-hand shouted. "Pardon the hounds, milord. They be harmless." The dogs fell back behind their master.

"Where's Toller?" Mort asked.

The stable-hand hung his head. "His back gave out summer last, milord. I be Harwood, and the stables be mine now."

"We'll need a cart and some animal to pull it," Mort said. "I'm not picky, but if it doesn't smell too badly, all the better."

"How far will your lordship be traveling?" Harwood asked.

"Bloody me, I don't know," Mort replied. "We're heading to Thunderglade."

Harwood let out a low whistle. "A far journey, milord. Three days on the road at best. Four if thy lady takes poorly to long stretches on a hard seat."

Mort waved away Harwood's concerns. "I'll have the beast back by nightfall, cart and all."

Esper cast the wizard a worried look. Images of careening along dirt trails in an ox-cart flashed in her imagination. Mort would have some clever way around them both being killed or thrown clear of the cart and would be all smug about it. The poor animal would be frantic, confused by its sudden transformation from plodding yoke-beast into a blur of legs and hooves.

"By what fell sorcery willest thou make such speed?" Harwood asked.

"The usual sort," Mort said. "And save the phony lingo for the tourists. You sound like a jackass. Just tell me how much it'll cost me to rent a cart and something willing to pull it."

Harwood sighed. "Eight pounds sterling. If you didn't exchange for coin-of-the-realm at the gift shop, we also accept hardcoin terras, jednu, arsicans, and xliknaar, as well as digital accounts from any certified ARGO bank. If you plan to use magic that affects any Harwood Stables property, I'm going to have to ask for an additional deposit of twenty pounds, and confirmation of membership in a recognized magical order."

"Toller didn't charge so much for a deposit."

"Toller went bankrupt and moved back to Luna."

Mort dug into the leather pouch tied to his belt and counted gold coins into Harwood's waiting hand. "I'll send someone to retrieve my deposit. But in the interest of playing your little charade, I'm not showing any proof of my affiliation. If you want to lodge a complaint, tell them the dark wizard Lord Mordred Pendergast defied you. See how far you get with that."

"You're... you're *the* Mordred?" Harwood asked. He backed a step away, even as Esper was climbing onto the front seat of a wagon that one of Harwood's boys had pulled around front.

Mort pulled himself onto the seat beside her and took the reins of a crotchety old mule. The beast brayed its annoyance as Mort tugged its head to the side and twisted to fix Harwood with a puzzled look. "I don't know how to take that question. Am I a semi-historical figure from two thousand years ago? No. Am I the bastard who bought Thunderglade Keep a few years back? Indeed I am."

With a snap of the reins, Mort urged the mule into forward motion. Esper surreptitiously gripped the seat with both hands, prepared for the mule to dart forward with supernatural speed at any moment. The wooden wheels rumbled along dirt ruts, keeping a sane and sensible pace until they were out of sight of the stables. A clopping of iron-shod hooves beat a counterpoint to the wheels. Esper was just relaxing her grip and settling in to enjoy a peaceful ride when both sounds faded away.

The cart kept moving. The change in elevation came so

subtly that Esper didn't take note of it at first, still puzzling over what Mort had done to quiet and smooth their ride. But by the time they were a meter off the ground it had become obvious that they would not be taking any more roads to reach Thunderglade. Esper renewed her grip on the seat with a fury.

"What are you doing?" Esper demanded. "There aren't even safety harnesses on this thing!"

Mort patted a gentle hand on her shoulder. "Relax. Science keeps its opinions quiet hereabouts. This little flight is no trouble at all. Safer than the *Mobius* for damn sure. Bakes my noodle every time I get to thinking about all the fell and tricksome sciences that all have to work just right for us not to suffocate or crash. It's amazing the thing can fly at all—just a bunch of nozzles shooting imaginary particulate to push it through air and space. This? Just clean, old-fashioned magic, like mother used to make."

Esper peered over the edge, and regretted it instantly. "It's got to be a hundred meters to the ground."

"Naw," Mort replied. "There isn't a meter within a hundred miles of here. They haven't been invented yet. Don't worry, though. You won't fall. Even if you did, you'd be fine. I'm betting you've got enough wizard in you by now that being unable to fathom the effects of a fatal fall like this would keep you from hitting hard enough to get seriously hurt."

"I what now?"

Mort put up his hands in defeat. Esper felt herself pressed firmly against the wagon seat. "Happy now?" The wagon performed a barrel roll. Esper screamed, but did not fall from her perch. "You can't fall out. Now sit back and enjoy the ride. It'll take a while to get there; my place isn't exactly on the beaten path."

Carl combed back his hair, flicking away the accumulated grease with each pass. Angling his head from side to side, he checked for signs of lingering blue. The vibrant, unnatural color had grown on him during his time in the Silde Slims race contest, making him stand out in a crowd. But that was the last thing he wanted to do right now. Now that he was back in the wizard's good graces, he could have asked Mort to undo the azrin swordmaster's curse and restore its original color, but then he'd have to get the wizard to put it back someday. Simpler was to just dye it to match the local style.

With a glance down at the datapad on his bed, Carl checked his reflection against the image of James Dean. The two of them looked nothing alike in the face, but he'd gotten the hair just about right. Combined with blue jeans and a plain white t-shirt, Carl looked like he belonged in the mid-twentieth century. He winked at the mirror and fired a finger blaster at his reflection.

The door to Carl's quarters opened as he was shrugging on his leather jacket. Black would have been a better fit, but his brown one would work fine on this world. "They here?" he asked.

"Tanny's letting them gawk at your new toy," Roddy replied. He referred to the stolen Squall in the cargo hold. The single-seat racing ship had been the coup from their last heist, worth over two million terras once they figured out a way to sell it.

"I'll be down in a minute," Carl said. "How do I look?" He turned toward the laaku mechanic and spread his arms.

"Like an idiot who should be holed up on an asteroid-mining platform in the middle of nowhere," Roddy said. "And not this playing dress up, time-traveling, rebel-without-a-cause bullshit. You're supposed to be dead; you think some hair dye is going to fool anyone?"

Carl pulled a pair of dark glasses from his pocket and put them on. He grinned.

Roddy just groaned, then turned and left.

Carl took off the glasses and doubled-checked the mirror one last time. He still looked like Carl Ramsey, winner of the Silde Slims Cadet Racer Challenge. But more importantly, he looked like someone who was *trying* to look like Carl Ramsey, but didn't have the blue hair for it. If anyone fingered him as the semi-famous pilot he had become, he'd admit to being an impersonator, or a fan, or maybe just tell people he heard that line a lot.

And if anyone really *did* recognize him... well, a guy couldn't stay dead forever.

Tanny had the cockpit canopy of the Squall open. She, Rhiannon, and the guy his sister was living with all had their heads poked over the edge, gawking inside. The sound of Carl's boots on the metal catwalk caught their attention.

"Hey, Squirt," Carl called down to them. Resisting the urge to hustle down the stairs, he kept up his cool demeanor and sauntered down to the cargo bay.

"Hey, Goofball... oh Lord," Rhiannon said. Her eyes followed him, wide and incredulous even as the rest of her face went slack. "What the hell are you supposed to be?"

"Incognito."

"This is New Cali, not a James Dean flick," Rhiannon said. She approached Carl and drew up short. With her jaw set, she relented and hugged him anyway.

"See?" Carl called to Tanny over his sister's head. "I got the look."

"I know you said not to sweat it, but I was still worried," Rhiannon said. She disentangled from her brother and punched him in the shoulder. "That's for being an ass. You haven't even told Mom and Dad?"

"You didn't explain?" Carl asked.

Tanny shook her head.

"Explain what?" Rhiannon asked.

Carl ignored the question and strutted over to the boyfriend. He was older, which was a change of pace for Rhiannon, tucked into an ash-gray suit that he seemed completely comfortable in. He had dark hair in a mid-twentieth business cut. Thin build. Light tan. The flat reflection off his horn-rimmed glasses meant that they were just a prop—like everything else on Peractorum when it came right down to it. "I'm Carl. You must be..."

"Lloyd Arnold," the boyfriend replied, sticking out a hand. "I've heard a lot about you."

"I was on holovid recently," Carl replied. "Everyone's heard a lot about me. You... I didn't know Rhi had broken up with Jesse until we landed here." He turned to Rhiannon. "What *did* happen between you and Jesse, anyway?"

It was Tanny's turn to punch Carl in the shoulder. Hers hurt worse.

"Where are Roddy and Mort?" Rhiannon asked, sidestepping Carl's rude questioning with a lifetime of practiced ease.

"Roddy's up in the common room," Tanny said. She hooked a thumb toward the stairs and addressed Lloyd. "I'll show you the way."

Rhiannon waited as Tanny and Lloyd left the cargo hold, saying nothing until the door closed behind them. "What is it?"

"You've got to talk to Mom and Dad," Carl said.

"Clue them in yourself, dead guy," Rhiannon retorted. "You owe them that much, at least."

Carl shook his head. "Out here I can keep it quiet. If I put a comm into Luna, I'm bound to snag a scan. Low tech is my friend right about now."

Rhiannon let out a beleaguered sigh that blew a lock of hair out of her face—one that had escaped imprisonment in hairspray. Carl flinched back, suddenly seeing his mother so clearly in his grown-up little sister. "What?" she demanded, noting Carl's reaction.

"You've turned into Mom," he replied. There had always been a resemblance, but twenty-odd years had made the distinction between them clear-cut. But most of his childhood memories were of his mother when she was about Rhiannon's age. The practical hairdo, the frumpy twentieth century duds, the little lines at the corners of her eyes—she was Becky Ramsey reincarnated.

"Better Mom than Dad," Rhiannon said. "Now cough it up. What couldn't you say in front of Lloyd?"

"We can't get the prize money from the race I won because Dad is suing Tanny over my estate," Carl said in hushed tones.

Rhiannon burst out laughing. "The two of you," she said, shaking her head. "I bet Dad knows you're alive, and he's just screwing with you."

"Nope," Carl said, jamming his hands into the pockets of his jacket. "Greedy old fucker already filed the suit. He wouldn't take a joke far enough to pay a lawyer."

"Tanny said the Squall was worth seven figures," Rhiannon said. "Maybe just let Mom and Dad keep the bread from the race and sell the racer?"

Carl poked a finger at his sister's nose, just like he'd done when she was little and talked back to him. "I don't *want* to sell the Squall. The prize money was so everyone got a cut of the job—a good one, too. Convince Dad to drop it and maybe I can cut *you* in on the take though. I'm guessing you're supporting Lloyd."

"Just until he passes the bar," Rhiannon replied. "He's coming at it from a history degree, not a law degree, which actually makes it easier around here."

"What does he play?"

"Golf."

"I mean what instrument."

"He doesn't," Rhiannon said. "He's an Ancient Americas whiz kid with a Yale sheepskin who got burnt out on the dork life. He came out here for a vacation, and I convinced him to stay."

"So you've had your first non-musician boyfriend," Carl said with a grin. "Rhi, you're finally growing up."

"Your turn next," she replied and headed for the stairs.

Dinner was ship-processed food, made to order. The sandwiches weren't bad, but they paled in comparison to the grilled burgers and hotdogs, the scents of which had pervaded Rhiannon's neighborhood. And while it would have been nice to have everyone trek out to New Cali for a backyard barbecue, Rhiannon had wanted to see Carl, and Carl was going nowhere for the time being. Tanny planned to make sure of that.

"So let me get this straight," Rhiannon said, dipping one of her identical, machine-extruded fries into a dollop of honey mustard. "You dropped a dime on the Poet Fleet for a heist you pulled and beat feet? Frosting pirates is gonna bite you in the ass one of these days."

"It was either that or dust a bunch of innocent miners," Carl replied with his mouth full. "I mean, we could have let Tanny's cousin Janice take the rap, but if we were willing to dangle her over the shark tank, we could have just cut and run. She wouldn't be the first member of the Rucker Syndicate to be outed as an *actual* criminal instead of a congenital suspect, but I wasn't going to be the one to do it. Tanny's family still considers me one of them."

"I liked the one where you rescued the kid from the dark science colony," Lloyd said. "No one gives those transgalactic corporations a second thought these days. I mean, human clones and no one spills it to the news outlets?"

Roddy made a rude, flapping noise with his lips. "How were we supposed to know the clone was acting funny? Like any of us knows how kids act. Mort's the only one with kids, and he hasn't seen 'em in forever."

"Mort's kids are my age by now," Rhiannon said. A thoughtful frown furrowed her brow. "Whoa, I guess they always *have* been about the same age as me."

"So where is this Mort?" Lloyd asked. "I've heard as much about him as I have Carl."

Tanny wondered about Lloyd. He was different from the vapid bad-boys Rhiannon generally took up with. He wore a business suit from the twentieth century like he had been wearing them all his life. His voice was calm. He spoke with a hint of an ivy-league accent. As far as Tanny had noticed he didn't have any body mods or cybernetic implants. But there was something glassy in his eyes; he didn't look right at anyone or make eye contact. Either he was on meds, or he had some sort of latent mental problem. Tanny couldn't decide which.

"We got a lead on the woman who kidnapped Kubu," Carl said. "Turns out, she's a laaku wizard."

"Bein' laaku's got nothing to do with it," Roddy muttered, sticking up for his species.

Carl let the laaku finish his grumbling and continued. "Anyway, the omni's all but blank on her, so we needed someone with connections to the Convocation who'll still deal with Mort. He took Esper with him out to Thunderglade to make contact."

"Ah, I'm hip," Rhiannon said. Her eyes widened, and she smiled impishly. "Mort's got himself an Esper."

"It's not like that," Tanny said.

"We think," Carl added.

"Who the hell knows," Roddy said, throwing back a beer.

"What I *do* know," Carl said. "Is that we're short on cash. Living might be cheap on this world, but fuel is fuel, and we're not going to get far if we don't alter our circumstances."

"As it stands, we're going to have to hitch a ride to pay for any rescue we make," Tanny said.

"I'll talk to the old man," Rhiannon said. "But you know how he can get."

"The three-month rule was *his idea*," Carl snapped. "How can he be pissed at me, just because he never ended up faking a death?"

"What about *your* old man, Tanny?" Rhiannon asked. "I'm sure he could spot you some green." It was an understatement. Don Rucker could have loaned them a mercenary escort.

Tanny shook her head. "No. The first debt we owe my father is the last time we're free to do our own thing."

Lloyd cleared his throat. Once he had everyone's attention, he looked to Rhiannon, who gave a slight nod. "I might be able to help."

Rhiannon stood and wrapped an arm around Lloyd.

"Lloyd's been helping get my career moving. We talked about this on the way over. Since this is one of the least greedy things I've ever heard of you guy doing, we'll lend a hand."

"Mostly terras," Lloyd said. "I'm not keen on the idea of breaking into a wizard's house and stealing a two-hundred kilo dog. We'll leave that part to you people."

"Or, you could just convince Dad to quit being an ass about the prize money," Carl said.

Rhiannon fixed Carl with a long-suffering look. Anyone who knew Carl long enough developed a version of it. "Don't bet on *that* happening."

The terror had worn off somewhere during the second hour. Rushing winds above the treetops weren't nearly as cold as they ought to have been. Far below, the countryside was green and alive. Villages dotted the landscape, interspersed with furrowed farmland and the occasional castle. Esper found herself staring over the side of the wagon, curiosity overcoming her fear of falling.

Pictures from agrarian worlds always showed vast stretches of farmland, crisscrossed by irrigation systems and swarming with picker drones. The farms below showed little order or planning. Here or there a farmhouse would sit beside a pasture and fields, and the spaces between them stayed wild and unplanted. Feeling brave, she rose up to get a better look directly below, leaning slightly—just slightly—over the side of the wagon. If she squinted, she could make out people down below.

"How's that?" Mort asked.

Esper twisted to look over her shoulder at the wizard, but

in doing so she made a key discovery. They were no longer flying level. There was nothing past Mort but the sun and sky, and when she looked back over the side, she realized that she was staring straight down with nothing between here and a kilometer drop. A scream escaped her and pierced the thin air.

"Put us back!"

"Why? We're almost there?" Mort asked calmly.

"Level," Esper shouted. "Put us back level!"

"Fine," Mort replied, resignation heavy in his voice. "You're no fun sometimes. You know that? Most magic I've used in months, and you want me to take the kettle off the fire."

Despite his annoyance, Mort righted the cart. The mule seemed oblivious to all the commotion. Esper found herself short of breath, her heart racing.

"Don't do that!"

"Do what?" Mort asked.

Esper spluttered, unable to put into words what ought to have been obvious.

"Don't help you out when you're trying to get a better view?" Mort asked. "Don't make sudden maneuvers while you're not paying attention?" He let his voice grow gravelly. "Don't use magic without asking you first?"

Suddenly the comforting force that had held Esper against her seat vanished. A chill ran through her as the realization struck her that only her own balance and grip were keeping her aboard the wagon. Panicked fingers latched onto the seat for the first time since shortly after they had taken to the air.

"Stop frightening me on purpose," Esper snapped. "You're not funny."

"One of these days you're going to figure out that you can stop me," Mort said. "I do it now because it's too easy. You ever see Roddy walk by an open bar and not grab a beer? Same thing."

"If this is what it's like being a wizard, I don't think I want to learn anymore," Esper said.

Mort harrumphed. "No, this is what it's like *not* being a wizard, at least when other people around you are. How pissed off was Carl before he decided he liked his hair blue? How doomed would you all be if I had an aneurysm while we were traveling the deep astral? Frankly, I marvel at how you people can stand being so helpless."

"We get used to it," Esper said dryly, still clutching the seat in a death grip.

"Well, we're just about there," Mort said. True to his word, Mort brought the wagon lower in the sky as they approached a village surrounding a small stone keep with a single spire sprouting from one corner. The village houses were simple like the ones by the stable. Smoke from cooking fires wafted from chimneys here and there. Mort guided them just above the rooftops, letting villagers spread word of their arrival via startled shouts and pointing.

They landed before a wrought iron gate twined so thick with ivy that no latch or hinge was visible. Once she and Mort were on solid ground, the mule took to the skies once more, pulling the wagon away without them. Esper watched it go, then turned her attention to the gate.

"Let me guess," Esper said. "The vines need magic to let us through."

"No," Mort said, scratching at his chin. "They ought to have fallen before the wrath of a diligent gardener. But clearly that has not been the case." With a wave of Mort's hand, the vegetation burst into flames.

Esper fell back and covered her nose and mouth with her

hand. The smoke still stung her eyes. "Watch it," she admonished.

"By gum, if you're still this helpless when we leave here, I'm signing on with a different ship," Mort said. He flicked his wrist, and a gale blew, dispersing the smoke. The gate swung open as well, though it seemed reluctant to give way before the magical wind. Rusted iron groaned in protest.

Beyond the gate, the courtyard was overgrown. Grasses grew as tall as Esper's waist, and there were shrubs and bushes sprouted up haphazardly across the landscaping. "You've really taken good care of the place," Esper said.

"I had this path cobbled when I bought the place," Mort muttered.

"Well, once again, I'm not dressed for this," Esper said. "I wouldn't make it three meters before I ruined this outfit."

Mort glanced her up and down, squinting one eye. She could envision the abacus within Mort's head, tallying and converting, figuring out how far three meters was. "No, I don't suppose you would." He took his staff in one hand and slammed the butt against the beginning of the path. Every bit of grass and shrub was flattened into a rough green carpet from the gate to the keep.

A trickle of villagers made their way to the gates of the keep. Many of them brandished tools, including one authentic-looking pitchfork. No one looked pleased to see them, but Mort didn't seem to notice. Esper caught him by the sleeve as he started down the garden path he'd just cleared.

"Mort, um, not to alarm you, but I think the peasants are revolting," Esper said quietly.

Mort snorted. "They're really not. Most of them are college educated. My *former* gardener had a PhD in botany. The local blacksmith taught Chaucer at Brown. They like the lifestyle, and not everyone aspires to be a—"

Esper swung the wizard around by his robe sleeve and pointed to the gathering crowd. "No, I mean rising up—and you darned well knew it. Do something."

"I was doing something," Mort replied. "We were going to head inside and see how bad things have suffered from their neglect. But since we've got them all right here..."

Mort turned to the villagers and spread his arms. They stopped, forming a wall of curious, grumbling onlookers. "People of Thunderglade, it is I, Mordred Pendergast, returned from my long absence. Since your abatement of taxes was contingent on upkeep of the grounds behind me here, I am declaring you all in default. We can figure out a payment plan, but I shall expect your first remittance by Wednesday the 7th. That gives you four days from today. If, by some chance, the grounds and keep are brought up to a livable and presentable standard in the interim, I may take that into consideration as a mitigating factor. Good day."

There were shouts and angry questions aimed in their direction, but Mort was already departing. Esper hurried along behind him and heard the iron gate slam shut as soon as she was clear of it.

The forest brush tugged and snagged at Kubu's shirt as he crashed headlong after the bunny, but nothing ripped. Not-Mommy said that Kubu didn't have to worry about his clothes ripping because they were made of good stuff. Clothes were still taking some getting used to; Kubu wasn't sure he liked them. In the mirror, he looked all grown up, and Not-Mommy was very firm that if people were going to treat him like a person and not a dog, he needed to wear them. But they made running feel funny, pulling on his knees and hips and stretching across his chest as he breathed hard. And the little flap... that was just plain inconvenient.

"He's right there!" Chimjo shouted, pointing behind a tree. Kubu's new friend was always trying to be helpful, but this time Kubu didn't need help. Of course the bunny had gone around the tree. Anyone with a working nose could smell right where it was. Kubu guessed the Chimjo had a bad nose like the other Roddy-people he'd met. They were little, with four feet that all worked like hands, and every one of them seemed very smart. Kubu supposed that having bad noses was a small price to pay for having four hands. Kubu would have settled for two that were good at gripping the ends of the string that pulled the little flap on his pants.

"You've got him now," Chimjo called out. The bunny darted for a hole beneath the roots of a tree, but Kubu was quicker. His teeth sank into the bunny's hindquarters. Its squeal of pain was brief; with a quick jerk of his head, Kubu brought it into his mouth, crunched once, and swallowed.

Kubu trotted over to Chimjo, licking the taste from his muzzle. Bunnies were yummy, and he had told Not-Mommy so. Ever since, he'd been eating two or three of them a day. When Kubu reached Chimjo, he got a disapproving look. "What's wrong?" Kubu asked.

Chimjo didn't have through-the-ear magic like Kubu did. Mort had put the magic through Kubu's ear so he could understand the silly noises people made. Chimjo never understood anything Kubu said, but he seemed to have a general idea this time.

"You got blood on your shirt," Chimjo said. "Mrs. Inviu isn't going to like that."

Kubu knew that was Not-Mommy's name, but the sounds were mushy and it was easier to think of her as Not-Mommy. It reminded him that she was not Mommy.

"Kubu!" Not-Mommy called from the house. It was a long ways off, and she had a little voice. But Kubu had good ears—better than Chimjo's, since the little Roddy-person didn't react to hearing the call.

"Kubu is coming," Kubu shouted back. He bounded off toward Not-Mommy's big house. It was much bigger than the flying house where Mommy lived; it was probably too big to fly. Chimjo followed, falling behind at every stride. He ran like Kubu, with four feet. Kubu had seen Roddy run that way a few times, but Roddy didn't run often. Chimjo ran to keep up with Kubu (or at least mostly keep up).

The grass was soft on Kubu's paws as he left the woods and made his way across the lawn. For all the dressing up Not-Mommy had subjected him to, Kubu hadn't been forced to wear shoes. There were more Roddy-people doing things like giving the bushes haircuts and driving little ships filled with things for the house. Not-Mommy was in charge of them, too.

"Kubu, look at the mess you've made," Not-Mommy said when he arrived at the front door. She always told him he was doing things wrong, even when he tried to do them the way she wanted. "Chimjo, take Kubu to change before dinner."

Despite the prospect of a change of clothes, Kubu perked up. Eating bunnies always made him hungry.

Dinner had ended and the night's entertainment turned its focus to beer. Lloyd and Rhiannon had brought some local brew that was supposed to be period-authentic, and the five of them shared stories as the sunlight glinting down from the overhead dome faded to moonlight.

"...and then he starts screaming at me in the middle of the hangar bay, with half the pilots and mechanics in the contest watching," Carl said with a grin.

"You're screwing with us," Rhiannon said. She stifled a belch and took another sip of her canned Olde America Lager.

"Nope, I was giving him every human slur I could think of," Roddy said. "No two ways; it happened just like that, except Carl was ready to bust a gut. Could have blown the whole scam. My backup plan if he did was to punch him below the belt."

They all laughed. It was almost loud enough to drown out the sound of the ship signaling an incoming comm.

"Shit," Tanny muttered. "I gotta go check on that. Could be from Silde Slims. You." She pointed a stern finger at Carl. "Zero decibels out of you. I don't want anyone picking up signs of you on a background recording."

Carl pinched his lips shut, spluttering laughter.

"I mean it!"

Carl nodded and sombered somewhat. Tanny started for the cockpit, then whirled on him and jabbed her finger his way once more. It wouldn't have been the first time she'd caught him making light of her precautions the instant her back was turned, but this time he showed every sign of contrition. Either he was wising up and waiting until she was out of sight, or he meant it this time.

Tanny settled herself into the pilot's seat and checked the comm panel. Fortunately, it was a publicly verified comm ID. Unfortunately it was Phabian Investigative Services, and they wanted voice.

Tanny grimaced as she keyed the comm. "This is Tania Ramsey, captain of the *Mobius*."

"Captain Ramsey," a laaku voice replied. It was still odd hearing that appellation applied to her. "I'm Agheli of Nen

Lian, Class 3 Fact Sifter for Phabian Investigative Services. Would you mind answering questions in cooperation with the investigation into the death of your late ex-husband, Bradley Carlin Ramsey?"

It was inevitable that they'd get to this point. Carl's faked death was suspicious from every angle. A race watched by a billion viewers, but no one saw a thing. A change of mechanics less than forty-eight hours prior to race time. Pilot error blamed for a crash by a pilot who'd spent three weeks showing those billion viewers that he could make a Squall dance like a puppet on strings. And that was all without considering the money involved. The quarter-million terra prize was more than anyone was willing to write off without an investigation.

"Of course," Tanny replied, hoping she hadn't hesitated noticeably. "Go ahead."

"Oh, we're not planning to conduct the investigation over public channels," Agheli said. "Your comm routing indicates you're on Peractorum. I can be out there with a team in seven hours. Please maintain your present location and await contact. Thank you for your cooperation."

The comm went dead. Agheli had closed the link.

Tanny sat staring at the comm panel for a long moment. They were coming. She'd been dreading the interview and police statement she knew would follow in the wake of Carl's apparent death. But a surprise inspection by Phabian's snoops? She leapt to her feet and ran.

"Went that well, did it?" Carl asked with a smirk as Tanny careened into the common room. He was sprawled across the couch with a beer can dangling from one hand. If it'd had anything left in it, it would have been pouring onto the floor.

"You've got to get out of here," she said. "They're coming."

Carl blew out a breath, puffing his cheeks. He blinked. "Well that's just unfortunate timing."

Tanny gaped at him. "How drunk *are* you?"

"Not so fly I can't drunk," he replied. She couldn't be sure if the slip was Carl just messing around or not.

"How long we got?" Roddy asked.

"Phabian Investigative Services said seven hours," Tanny replied. "But I'm not betting against them being early. If *I* worked intel, I'd stake someone out, *then* tell them I was coming."

Rhiannon pushed her chair back from the table. "And this is where we split. It's been fun catching up. I'd almost forgotten what it was like having Johnny Law kill a meal. I'm sure they'll be dropping in on us, too."

"Sorry," Tanny said.

Rhiannon patted Lloyd on the cheek. "It's copacetic. And Lloyd's practically a lawyer, so I think he can figure out how to keep us out of the pokey. Goodnight."

"See ya, Squirt," Carl said, saluting with his empty beer can.

"Just don't ditch the scene before I get to see Mort," Rhiannon said. She gathered Lloyd and left.

"Well, we're a little fucked," Roddy said. "Mr. Plan-From-Hell here's been getting DNA all over things for days."

"At least he's *supposed* to have DNA all over the ship," Tanny replied. "We just need to get rid of any recent traces. Shower. Bedsheets. Laundry." She grabbed the can from Carl's hand. "Empties."

"I'll take the Squall," Carl said. "Hide out at the edge of the colony for a few days."

"Brilliant plan, Peachfuzz," Roddy said. "Except me and Tanny were pretty much already assuming that part. What we gotta worry about is the trail you leave behind."

"Tow the Squall across the field," Tanny said. "The grav

sled can handle the weight, and it won't leave a residue of ion wash in the cargo hold."

Roddy pointed to Tanny, but looked Carl's way. "See? That's planning."

"Maybe you should find Mriy instead of sticking around here," Tanny said.

He waved his hands in front of his face. "No way; no pay. I had my fill of that kung-fu samurai fencing bullshit. Got cursed last time, remember?" He sat up, wobbling slightly.

There was a greasy smear on the arm of the couch where Carl's head had rested. "And we've gotta clean off anything his head's touched."

"I'll just find a quiet place a few hundred kilometers from here," Carl said. "I'm already dressed for the colony, and I know the lingo. I can fit in like a resident hitchhiking from town to town. Ten million people live here; it's not like they all know each other."

"Fine," Tanny said. "Get going as soon as we pack a bunch of your personal shit up in that toy raceship of yours."

"Pray that no one's stargazing tonight," Roddy said. "There may not be orbital traffic control around here, but you don't want some amateur astronomer finding something suspicious in the skies. These chuckleheads would put it in the papers as a UFO sighting. Every bloody one of them's traveled on a starship at some point in his life, and they still can't get enough of fucking UFO sightings."

"I'll keep it below the radar, chief," Carl said with a sloppy salute.

Tanny shot Roddy a worried look. "We can't send him up like this, can we?"

"Sister, it's either send him as is, or retrofit a star-drive to that Squall in the next couple hours," Roddy said. "Let's pump him full off coffee and start cleaning."

Fact Sifter Agheli arrived two hours ahead of his estimate. Whether it was through fortunate circumstances or intentional dissembling (fact sifters never "lied"), he had not caught Tanny and Roddy by surprise. The *Mobius* had been scrubbed and tidied, stripped of recent evidence of Carl's habitation.

Roddy had split off from the cleaning and taken the star-drive apart. Under the guise of a complete overhaul, he'd reduced it to individual components spread out across the cargo bay floor—not coincidentally covering the area where the Squall had been stored. There were odd bits of magic that were part and parcel to the system, their function a matter for more scrambled minds than his own to untangle. Roddy knew how to clean them, align them, and secure them within the device, but not a damn thing about how to operate them. But as a matter of good faith, it was hard to beat a stripped-down star-drive for convincing the authorities that they weren't going to run.

There weren't many starships that could outrun one of Phabian Investigative Services' corvettes in astral space, let alone without using a star-drive.

The fact sifter was tall for a laaku, a full head taller than Roddy. His fur was gray at the cheeks and chin, his brow prominent. The dusky gray Investigative Services uniform he wore hadn't a wrinkle upon it, and aside from rank insignia, it bore a patchwork of commendations and certifications over the left breast. He carried his datapad like a loaded blaster. A real pro.

With a quick glance at the datapad, Agheli greeted Roddy at the cargo ramp. "You must be Rodek of Kethlet. Thank you for your cooperation at this late hour local time."

"My mom doesn't even call me Rodek anymore. I go by Roddy. I'm a night person anyway; come on in."

"Is the captain available?" Agheli asked. He stepped aboard, followed by two assistants: a human and another laaku. The human carried a bulky scanner. It was going to be one of *those* inspections.

"Yeah, lemme grab her," Roddy said. But in this case, "grabbing" was just hitting the nearest comm panel. "Yo, sleeping beauty, the inquisition is here." He turned off the comm with the butt of his fist.

Agheli gave him a disapproving frown. "This isn't an inquisition. We're here to collect facts surrounding the investigation of Bradley Ramsey's death. Fact sifters are scattered across the galaxy right now doing likewise. Currently, we have no reason to question your alibi."

Roddy sighed. "Sorry, buddy. My best friend dies, and next thing I know, I got vultures circling. I'd cleaned up my act, but this set me back drinking again." He pulled a can of Earth's Preferred from his coveralls and popped it open, taking a long drink.

"Once we're done here," Agheli's laaku tech said, "I can get you on the list at a psychological detox clinic. Those bloodstream cleansers are a scam. Doesn't stop you from getting pulled right back in."

"Thanks, pal," Roddy said, taking another drink. The prick. Maybe *he* didn't know how to enjoy himself, but Roddy did.

The door to the common room opened. "Sifter Agheli," Tanny said. "Nice to meet you." Her hair was mussed from recent contact with a pillow, but she was fully clothed. She'd have been down to the cargo bay quicker if she didn't have to make it look like she'd been sleeping when Roddy commed.

"You as well," Aghlei replied. "Pleasantries concluded. Let us begin. Captain Ramsey, I will need your ship's logs and sensor database. Rodek, please escort my techs through the ship, rendering whatever assistance they require."

Wonderful. Not only were they planning to scan the *Mobius* down to the rivets, they expected him to pitch in to help. "Sure thing, boss."

"These records are atrocious," Agheli said, horror echoing in his voice. "How do you people operate a business this way?"

"Do we *look* like we're successful?" Tanny asked. "Besides, we specialize in discretion; same code of ethics as an independent investigators-for-hire. Once we receive final payment on a job, we scorch the records on it."

"You realize I can't help but find that highly suspicious," Agheli said. "My job is to collect facts—facts related to criminal investigations. In my professional experience, falsified and destroyed records are nearly always a sign of illegal conduct."

"You can find me suspicious all you want," Tanny replied. "We don't make what we do much of a secret. We mostly operate out in border space or around unsanctioned colonies outside ARGO jurisdiction. Maybe the money isn't consistent, but we don't get buttoned up in little uniforms anymore." She poked a finger at Agheli, but stopped short of touching him. "If we hadn't been so hard-scrabble the last couple months, Carl wouldn't have bothered with that contest."

"Yes... the Silde Slims Cadet Racer Challenge," Agheli said. "Mr. Ramsey made quite a commotion in the racing community, didn't he? As far as you knew, was he planning on sharing the race winnings with the rest of his crew?"

"Yeah," Tanny replied. "I mean, you hear stories about guys getting greedy and taking it all for themselves, but that wasn't Carl's style. If he wanted to make big money, he'd have easier ways than trying to disappear on us with 250k terras."

"Please elaborate," Agheli said, making notes on his datapad.

Tanny shrugged. "If you're any kind of fact sifter, you already know who my father is. Don Rucker owns a good chunk of Mars. He *liked* Carl. It's that whole brash, flippant, tough-guy thing fighter pilots get good at, and Carl's great at it. My dad was a sucker for it, too. Standing job offer any time Carl wanted it. But that wasn't his style—it's not *our* style. We might travel on the edge of law and order, but we live strictly on the law-abiding side."

"I see..."

Tanny scratched at the back of her neck and continued. "I mean, we do stumble into shit now and then. Hadrian IV... once we figured what was going on there, we contacted the One Church to send humanitarian aid."

Agheli tapped at his datapad for a moment. "I'm not familiar with the incident you mentioned."

Tanny waved a dismissive hand. "You'll look it up later. Just know: that was us. We did what anyone with a sense of conscience would have had to do there. Kidnapping sentients to display in a zoo?" She shook her head and shuddered, hoping she wasn't overdoing it.

The questioning went on for another hour and a half. The fact sifter delved into her rocky relationship with Carl, her actions and whereabouts leading up to the events in the final race of the Silde Slims contest, and Carl's known associates. The crew had gone over the story they'd use for the authorities, knowing that an investigation was bound to catch up with them, but it was still exhausting to lie throughout an entire conversation. If Agheli were secretly running a truth scan on her, it would have failed for lack of a baseline reading.

"As for the remainder of your crew, where might I find them?" Agheli asked. It was a signal flare that he was finally finished with her.

"It was just me and Roddy here when you commed," Tanny replied.

Agheli held up a placating hand. "Of course. I didn't expect you to produce them on short notice. But I do expect you to provide their present whereabouts."

"They're big boys and girls," Tanny said. "I don't keep a tracker on them. Mort and Esper went to New Camelot. Mriy is touring the Celestial Empire. They'll meander back here eventually, but they're not on a schedule—or a leash."

"I see..." Agheli replied with a frown.

After an awkwardly interventionist first impression, Roddy found himself taking a liking to Maikai—Mikey—of Zenlon. The laaku inspector, unlike so many to look over the *Mobius* before him, seemed to grasp the beauty of an ugly ship.

"Can't say I'd have used an aqua-ski engine to recycle the ship's air," Mikey said as he closed the access panel. "Why the extra joules?"

"Needed it," Roddy replied. "The base model was a diplomatic shuttle. Life-support designers assumed it would be landing on A-tech planets. We land in enough shitty atmospheres that I had to triple the filtering. Stock O2 pump would have been like breathing through a tube."

The life-support systems were a wild card. If Mikey was crazy-good at his job, the laaku might have been able to piece together a DNA profile of the recent occupants of the ship based on residue in the air filtration system. There just hadn't been the time to completely scrub a system that ran throughout the entire ship. The lucky break was that Carl's DNA *should have* been all over the place—just not recent samples.

Mikey jerked a thumb at the human tech, and the big oaf hefted the access panel back into place. Roddy had caught that the human's name was Gustavson, but the guy had hardly said a word through the whole inspection. As far as Mikey seemed concerned, Gustavson was just a portable pair of arms.

"Let's go have a look at those crew quarters," Mikey said. They had already inspected five of the six rooms the crew used for sleeping and personal effects. He had diverted them away from Mort's room before either of the inspectors set foot inside. "I backed up my data to my ship. Anything goes wrong in your wizard's room, Investigative Services will cover the cost of new scanning equipment."

"Won't cover the cost of you, though," Roddy said glumly. He'd hoped that like so many inspectors before him, Mikey would be dissuaded from risking his A-tech poring over wizardly trappings. But unlike most of those others, Mikey was ready to let everything get scrambled in an effort to be thorough.

Mikey paused. "This wizard of yours... some kind of psychopath?"

Yes. Roddy wanted to just out and say it. Mort was a brutal killer on the run from the Convocation for two decades with a trail of bodies in his wake. "Naw, just don't trust a thing in there, personally. If you gotta go in, just watch yourself. I'll be standing outside."

"Maybe we ought to—" Gustavson began.

"Quiet," Mikey snapped. "We're going to do our job. Wizards aren't dangerous to creatures of pure science. My own unwavering belief in the laws of physics will protect me. Wizarding is all about belief."

Roddy shrugged. It was a nice way to go through life, if you could keep out of sight of *real* wizards. He tended to doubt that Mikey believed in science half as much as Mort believed against it. They traipsed through the cargo hold, past Roddy's dismantled star-drive, and through the common room.

"Shame we're on a tight schedule," Mikey said. "Wouldn't mind getting a look around this backwater. It's like a museum full of living people. Humans... am I right? Go figure." He chuckled, drawing a grunt from Gustavson. "Aw, can it, ya big baby. Can't take a little joke at the expense of your dopey DNA cousins? It's not like I lumped *you* in with those retroverts. *You've* got half a brain in that oversize skull of yours."

Roddy stepped in front as they reached Mort's quarters, resting a hand on the door handle. "Last chance to back off. Our wizard knows his shit. If he wanted stuff hidden, you wouldn't find it in there if you stood on it."

Mikey narrowed his eyes. "That some sort of coded clue?"

Roddy clenched his feet into fists, trying not to match the gesture with his hands. It was a giveaway of stress if Mikey was looking down; even Gustavson probably knew it, working on Phabian. For all the inconvenience of his presence, Roddy didn't want to see either of the two inspectors get hurt. Knowing he'd be gone for days or weeks and that an investigation was a possibility, who knew what Mort might have done in there.

"No. Just trying to get through to you that your best-case scenario is finding nothing," Roddy said. He needed a beer, but the last thing he wanted was another lecture from Mikey. If it might have stopped the laaku inspector, he'd have given it a shot. But say this for Miakai of Zenlon: he was a professional.

"Thanks, pal," Mikey said. "We'll be careful." With that, Mikey stepped aside and let Gustavson precede him into Mort's quarters.

A part of Roddy wanted to linger at the doorway. It was the same part that watched races for the chance to see a crash, or eavesdropped on Carl and Tanny when they were fighting. But in this case, there was no holovid to protect him from speeding shrapnel, no intervening wall to keep him from being noticed. If Mort rigged up something to suck intruders into an extra-spatial vortex, or to summon a ravenous swarm of teaspoon-sized demons to devour them, he wanted no part of it.

He cracked open a beer and waited.

Agheli and Tanny returned from the cockpit. "Where are my inspectors?" Agheli asked. By the look on Tanny's face, she had weathered quite a storm.

"Checking out the ship's wizard's room," Roddy replied. He noted the sour look Agheli gave his beer can. "What? Ain't illegal here. If you want to file it in your report, file it. Next time I visit the home world I'll know to look over my shoulder for substance abuse enforcement."

"I'd prefer you sober for your deposition," Agheli said.

"That hull breached the night I heard about Carl," Roddy said. "Ain't putting air back in it now." To emphasize his point, he took another drink. "Go ahead and ask away." He wasn't afraid of a few questions. As far as he knew, Carl *was* dead. The idiot had a few beers in him before he took off in the stolen Squall. Odds were decent that he'd slammed it into a diner or a movie theater, or some other primitive local structure.

The door to Mort's quarters opened.

All eyes turned to the two inspectors. "We found nothing," Mikey said.

"Nothing," Gustavson echoed.

"Very well then," Agheli said with a curt nod. "Return to the ship. I'll be along once I've interviewed Mr. Rodek."

"We did a thorough and complete job to the best of our abilities," Mikey said. His voice was mechanical, with awkward pauses after each word like he was reading from a script.

"I concur," Gustavson said. "We did our jobs well and found nothing. There is nothing further to investigate." He had the same odd cadence to his speech.

"Yes, yes. Now off with you," Agheli said, shooing them away with a flick of his wrist.

Roddy hid his smirk behind a beer can. It was probably going to be the last amusement he'd have until Agheli was gone, so he enjoyed it while he could.

The comm system was shut down. External lights were off. He wasn't running anything but close-range sensors—strictly on passive scan. Cruising along at speeds never exceeding a couple hundred klicks, he had the ion signature of a harvest drone—a compromise that Peractorum made with modern science because so few people moved to a retrovert colony to do backbreaking manual labor. Carl's Squall was incognito and content to stay that way.

Carl was incognito as well, still dressed in his old-Earth finest, blue hair concealed under thick layers of dye and grease. That part was lucky. Being chased off the *Mobius* on short notice would have been a lot more awkward without a disguise. The four beers—or was it five?—before he left were less helpful. In the dark, on an unfamiliar world, he had no idea where he was heading.

There was moonlight to see by. The ground was washed-out colors, but it showed the contours Carl needed to navigate around. The Squall handled sluggishly, reacting a fraction of a second after he wanted it to. It was amazing that the pile of bolts had won him a race, considering the trouble he was having with it.

Most of the countryside he flew over was undeveloped. Grassy plains, stretches of forest, a few shrimpy mountains or good-sized hills, depending on which way you looked at them. Here and there, he'd pass over a road, or see lights from a city—if you could call them that—on the horizon. But he wasn't looking for a city right then. He wasn't sure what he was looking for, other than a good night's sleep, a place to take a leak, and maybe find some eggs and bacon in the morning. This seemed like the sort of world where he could manage all three just about anywhere. But first he was going to need to make up his mind and put the Squall to bed somewhere safe.

Swooping in low, Carl followed a major highway. It was the middle of the night, and late-night traffic didn't fit with the vibe of the colony. Skimming along a meter off the ground on repulsors, he might as well have been in a Chrysler or a Chevy, out for a joyride. The way he was dressed, it should have been a motorcycle. There was a split just ahead, guarded by a billboard nestled among tall bushes. Carl fired forward thrusters and came to a stop close enough to read it by the moonlight.

WELCOME TO THE FUTURE SITE OF LION ESTATES

BREAKING GROUND - MARCH 2561

LOTS STILL AVAILABLE. CONTACT GRACIE REAL ESTATE.

Carl did some quick math in his head and concluded that March was months away. This terraformed world didn't have its own calendar, so it must have been synced with Earth Standard. A few months was plenty of time. He swung the Squall around and lodged it in the shrubbery behind the billboard.

The night air was cool. Sobering. It felt good in a clean, unprocessed sort of way. After a half kilometer walking along the side of the road, feeling the soft squish of soil beneath his boots, Carl decided where he drew the line on being at one with nature, and continued his journey afoot from atop the asphalt. The direction he chose was at random. Or at least, it was the direction he'd been going in the Squall, so he continued along that general line on foot.

Time passed weirdly with no way to mark it. Carl hadn't brought a datapad, or anything else that might have seemed out of place in the twentieth century. He didn't own a watch appropriate to the time period. There were no overhead signs, no clock towers, not even passers-by to ask. Left. Right. Repeat. He couldn't remember ever having been awake for a hangover to set in before. It was looking like this was going to be his first, as the sky ahead hinted at a coming dawn.

Behind him, the hum of an engine approached. A truck was headed Carl's way, its headlights shining in his eyes. Shielding his eyes with one hand, he waved the other overhead, signaling the vehicle. At the last moment, he had the presence of mind to quickstep out of the middle of the road.

The truck slowed down and stopped with a squeak of brake pads. The motor continued to run, chugging at the front and belching a fog of exhaust out the back. The side of the truck was painted, declaring it to belong to the *Harksville Gazette*. "Hey there, friend. Need a lift?"

The driver was a middle-aged man, gray-haired with a youthful face. The sort of man who did a menial job because he loved it, cheerful even in the pre-dawn hours. It was a gold strike, a straight flush, an oil gusher in a pauper's yard. "Thanks, pops. My dogs have had it," Carl said, trying his best to keep to the lingo. He opened the passenger door and climbed aboard. As he sank into the seat, his back informed him that he should have given it a rest hours ago.

"I didn't see a car," the driver said. "How'd you get way out here?"

"My old lady kicked me out," Carl said. It was the truth, from a certain point of view. "Now I'm just looking to hit the next town. I'm Dick Derringer." He stuck out a hand, which the driver shook without hesitation.

"Pete Mulrooney. Nice to meet you. Hey, any chance that's Derringer like the singer?"

Dumb. He hadn't thought up an alias ahead of time, and now he was named after a guy that this world knew better than he did. It was one thing slipping Hendrix and Jagger past clueless officers on the border space patrols. He was going to need a new alias once he got rid of Pete. "That's Rick Derringer," Carl said. "My folks were big fans. Called me Richard, but I go by Dick instead."

"Got a place to stay when you get where you're headed?" Pete asked. "Don't mean to pry, but you don't look like you planned this out ahead of time."

"Brother, you don't know the half of it," Carl said. "I was flying on fumes. Figured I'd stop in the first diner I came across and have a few cups of coffee." The thought of buying coffee drew Carl's thoughts to one key oversight. He patted at his pockets. Not only was he broke in local currency, but he didn't even have hardcoin terras on him. And he was in no position to take funds out of any digital account, either. Dead men have lousy credit.

Pete looked over as Carl's realization struck. Carl wasn't

used to being so transparent, but he was in no condition to play it cool—despite being dressed for the part. "You haven't got a dime, have you, son?"

"My... uh, my old lady..."

"Yeah, I hear you," Pete said. "Been ridin' solo going on ten years now myself. Lemme make you a deal. You help me unload these papers once we get to Anaheim, and I'll buy you a cup of joe and a plate of hash browns."

"Make it bacon and eggs, and you've got yourself a deal."

Esper woke to the musty smell of a room too long closed up. If she had realized that they weren't going to be spending the night in the village, she'd have focused her attention on airing out the guest rooms and laundering the bedclothes. Mort had proved that there were limits to his magic—he couldn't clean if his life depended on it. The spells layered over the keep had kept it from rot and infestation, but little else.

Her borrowed bedroom was walled in stone, dark gray granite with a texture that felt rough but looked smooth. No mortar sealed the stone blocks together, but not a sliver of light passed through from the outside. The exception was the stained glass window that depicted a scene of a lone tower upon a hilltop, and two smaller windows of clear glass. The edges of the stonework were carved in bas-relief, with dragons chasing knights, knights hunting stags, stags following maidens, and maidens riding dragons, all in an endless loop. If the carvings held any significance, their meaning escaped her.

There was no bath, and she hadn't brought a change of clothes. Donning her dusty, scuffed dress from the day before, Esper headed downstairs to find Mort.

She found the wizard in the grand parlor, asleep in an armchair. Slouched down, robe and hair both rumpled, he hardly looked like the lord of a village keep. Esper wasn't quite sure she believed it herself. It was the twenty-sixth century, well past the age when hereditary nobles ruled anything more than the occasional late-hour talk vid. But Thunderglade and the rest of New Camelot didn't want to be a part of the twenty-sixth century. They were some muddled up mix of the Dark and Middle Ages.

Mort shifted in his sleep, and Esper flinched. She'd awakened him once before, when the circumstances were dire. Without her life in the balance, it seemed more prudent to leave him be. She turned and tiptoed from the room, but only got as far as the door.

"Lady Richelieu?" Mort asked with a yawn. "What are you doing here?"

"I was just going to look for some breakfast."

Mort waved a hand. "No, not that. Why are you still on the grounds? I sent you away."

Esper took a step back. "Mort. This is Thunderglade. We arrived last night. The last thing you said to me was to watch out for gargoyles."

Mort blinked and rubbed his eyes. "Oh. Yes. Sorry. Hope they didn't bother you during the night. Ornery creatures."

"And you didn't send me away?" Esper said.

Mort stood and stretched with an audible crackling of stiff joints. "And clean this place up myself? Our guest will be here in hours—give or take a few hours."

"Can you finally tell me who it is that we're expecting?"

"And spoil the surprise?" Mort asked. He was beginning to sound like himself again, full of snark and vinegar.

"Yes!"

Mort shuffled over to the window, still stiff and slow.

When he threw back the heavy drapes, the dim parlor was washed in morning sunlight. "Fine. Have it your way. We're meeting Keesha Bell."

Esper frowned. She'd heard that name before. But where? Then it came to her. "She's the one who got us that egg-delivery job."

"Not exactly," Mort said. "She got us the contact who got us the job. She just thought of us when she had something on her plate that didn't fit her business."

"What business would that be?"

"She's a collector of this and that," Mort said. "Some she keeps, some she sells. She's made herself quite a living at it. But in this case, she's got enough of a network that she can make inquiries without raising too many questions."

"How can you ask questions without making them?" Esper asked before she stopped to think. This was entirely the sort of flippant, irrelevant question that Mort could follow for hours, off on a journey to the far end of a tangent.

But Mort just grinned. "Point taken. She can seek answers to her own questions without inspiring them within others. And never underestimate the value of precise language. Intentional misinterpretation is a key form of argument. It's good to practice it. And it's better practice for avoiding those traps yourself. People can't take what you say the wrong way if you give it to them flawlessly formed."

"So Keesha Bell is going to tell us where Kubu is being held?" Esper asked, steering them back onto the conversation's original course.

"Already found that out," Mort said. "That's not the tricky part. This Inviu of Chapath, she's a wizard. Being laaku, that doesn't frighten me. I'm sure I could flatten her like a house of cards in a thunderstorm. But what else has she got going on? Laaku aren't known for shunning tech, not even their wizards. They might not know a screw from a bolt—"

"They're pretty much the same thing," Esper interjected, thanks to Roddy's crash course in ship maintenance.

"But they don't mind employing people who do, and living with sciencey stuff all around them. She's sure to have taken precautions to guarantee her own safety."

"Maybe not everyone's as paranoid as you," Esper replied.

"Most aren't," Mort said. "Many are dead. The rest are the ones to worry about. Now let's get this place presentable. I didn't know when I invited her here that it was in shambles."

Esper didn't say it. She wanted to, just to show Mort she'd picked up on it. He'd deny it, most likely, because he denied just about anything she puzzled out about him. But he was in a tizzy over making a good impression. This was the same wizard who wore a sweatshirt until the accumulated stains made it too stiff to pull over his head in the morning. The same wizard who only shaved when the scruff of his beard grew itchy. And now he was dusting furniture and trimming the garden paths? Mort was looking forward to seeing Keesha Bell for more than just information.

Sharky's Pool Hall was lit by fluorescent bulbs in hooded awnings over each billiard table. Back lit smoke wafted from cigarettes and cigars. Every few seconds, a crack would sound from one table or another as phenolic resin balls collided. Players jawed at one another, boasted over victories, and called their shots. Ice clinked in glasses of various liquors. Paper currency rustled as it changed hands. Some of that currency was counted into Carl's waiting hand.

"Double or nothing?" Carl offered. The gentleman in the shabby suit gave him a glare and walked away. Forty bucks wasn't going to lose anyone his house, but it was sure to pay for a few nights in a hotel, a nice meal or three, and maybe a change of clothes. "Your loss, buddy."

He had arrived mid-morning to a deserted room, barstools set upside down on tables and the bar. It was the middle of nowhere, halfway between Anaheim and San Jose, and the trucker traffic hadn't picked up for the day. One of the bartenders had been cleaning the floors, and Carl offered him a hand in exchange for a couple practice games on the house. It had been years since he'd played, but there had been a few pool tables in the rec room aboard the *ENV Justiciar*. By the time the early crowd had arrived, two things had become clear. Carl had managed to get most of the rust scraped off his game, and most of the patrons of Sharky's didn't know the game worth a damn.

It was the faux-tourist thing popping up again. The stiffs who lived in New Cali just wanted the sniff, not the swallow. They came in and plunked money down on the table like it was the fare to a roller coaster or admission to a movie theater. For five or ten minutes at a pop, they got to feel like bad boys. Of course they weren't all horrible, and Carl lost a game here and there; there were at least two other guys at Sharky's hustling the rubes. But by tacit agreement, they stayed out of each other's way and kept on winning. Carl was beginning to wonder why he bothered running a starship at all.

"Who's got next?" he called out. A few heads turned, gave him a wary look, then turned back. Drinkers. Spectators. What he needed were players. "C'mon. Friendly game?"

Carl managed to get in a few rounds of nine-ball with no stakes, but that wasn't helping his bankroll. Who knew how long he'd have to play Chet Diamond, his new alias. The more he could rack up to pad his pockets, the less chance he'd have to resort to honest work. Pete the newsman might have slipped him a couple bucks for bus fare in exchange for help with his morning route, but that wasn't how Carl wanted to spend his time on the lam. If he was supposed to be dead, then this was sort of like an afterlife. He'd be damned if he was going to spend his afterlife breaking his back lugging stacks of newspapers.

Finally some lively marks walked in. It was after dark, and Carl was running on a belly full of cheap beer and greasy bar food. If the fellas in the patched denim jackets and bandannas were anything like what they were pretending to be—a gang of no-goodnik bikers—then they'd be game.

"Howdy, strangers," Carl called out. He raised a hand and gave a twitch of a wave, leaning up against the table he'd claimed for most of the day. "You here to drink, play, or do a little of both?" He raised a brown bottle of beer to his lips to make the point that both was his style.

"How come I never seen you around here?" one of the bikers replied, his voice bellowing out for the whole pool hall to hear. He was the biggest of the lot, beer-bellied and bearded, with his jacket torn off at the sleeves to make a ragged vest. "And you callin' me stranger?"

"I travel a lot," Carl said, smiling. "Every place I go's full of strangers. Got nothing against strangers though. You game?"

Every bar and pool hall had regulars. They had a way of acting more at home than the owners did. Up until now, Carl hadn't been able to pick out any true regulars at Sharky's. But these bikers owned the place. It was time to dig a little deeper into his pockets, up his game, and squeeze these road-pilots for all they were worth.

"Sully, hand over Emma Lou," the biker said to the bartender. In nine hours of loitering, Carl hadn't picked up on the bartender's name. But Sully ducked behind the bar and came up with a long, narrow case and handed it over to one of the lead biker's companions. Inside was a pool cue, disassembled, and the assistant biker turned it into its weaponized form for his boss. "Whadda they call you?" he asked Carl.

"Chet Diamond," Carl replied, touching a finger to his temple in a piss-poor salute. "How 'bout yourself? You seem like top dog around here. You got a name?"

"Call me Panhead," he replied. He sauntered over to Carl with Emma-Lou in hand and a glass mug of draft beer that someone pressed into his hand as he passed by. He took down the entire mug in one long pull, gasping at the end. "And you're in a heap of trouble, pardner."

Carl racked up a game of nine-ball. "Go ahead and break. Ten bucks a game." He slapped a ten-dollar bill onto the side of the table.

"We don't play for sissy money around here," Panhead said. Hoots and encouragement from his gang echoed the sentiment. "Twenty's the least I'll take out Emma Lou for. And since she's already out, you better be willing to play."

"I was just being neighborly, offering a warm-up game," Carl replied, fishing in his pocket and adding a pair of fives to his ten.

Panhead grinned, showing off a missing front tooth. He pulled out a roll of bills from the inside pocket of his vest. Sliding out a single bill, he mashed it down onto the edge of the table with a greasy hand. Carl fixated on the roll of bills as it disappeared back to the sweat-stained interior of that vest. There had to have been thousands there. He wouldn't risk trying to bankrupt Panhead, but the guy could afford to lose a few hundred without getting bent out of shape over it.

The biker walked around to the head of the table and broke with a thunderous crash. Balls scattered, but none went in. Carl took his turn and dropped the 1 and 2 balls before missing a shot. Panhead sank the 3, but then left Carl the 4, 5, and 6 balls, before Carl made a combination shot to sink the 9.

"Nice game," Carl said, scooping up Panhead's money from the table but pointedly leaving his own bet in place.

"Lemme have another shot," Panhead insisted. Carl wasn't going to dissuade him. "Forty this time."

With a shrug, Carl added Panhead's losses from the previous game to his own bet. "Sure thing, pal. Just gimme a minute."

Grabbing his winnings, Carl headed for the men's room. This was a setup. Nobody played like Panhead did, not if he owned his own cue with a name and everything. The increase in the bet size was his cue to leave. Panhead was going to hustle him. No one got to be a con man without learning the other guys' tricks. Carl wasn't good enough to hustle pool, but he sure knew what a hustle looked like. He could always play the line a little longer and call it a night just before Panhead pulled the rope and let the guillotine drop on him. It was a retrovert colony, for God's sake; it wasn't like they were going to have *real* criminals. Panhead and his boys weren't going to dust him over a game of pool. Hell, the whole point of "dusting" someone required energy weapons or magic, neither of which fit the vibe in this colony.

The men's room was everything Carl had hoped for. A single urinal and toilet, a sink, and a window that opened to the outside. There was something undignified about climbing through a window and skulking off into the night. It didn't fit with the slick-back hair and jeans-and-leather look. But Carl was a realist—that look was as phony as the rest of the colony. He was a twenty-sixth-century guy. Maybe he liked the music and a few of the old flatvids from the era, but he didn't owe twentieth century "cool" a damn thing.

Carl flipped the little metal hook on the door into the loop on the doorjamb. It would stop anyone entering inadvertently and stop exactly no one over the age of five from breaking in. The window opened easily. With the toilet for a stepladder, he'd be able to make it out with little difficultly or dignity. His jacket would get in the way, so—

His jacket. Carl wasn't wearing it. It hung from a peg on the wall next to the spare cue sticks. He'd taken it off shortly after arriving at Sharky's and had hardly given it a thought since. There was always a chance he could come back for it. And worst case, he could always buy a new one. But he'd stolen that jacket years ago—or at least found it and never looked for the owner. It had a story. It had character. It was an old friend.

Carl closed the window and headed back out into the pool hall.

"Rack 'em up," he called out, snatching up the cue he'd left outside the men's room door.

"Your break, pal," Panhead said. He waved a meaty hand at the table, where one of his lackeys was racking a fresh array of nine balls.

Carl spared a quick glance at the scrawny biker with the Earth Marines tattoo on his shoulder. He didn't want to get a loose rack, but the guy was making sure all the balls were touching. Unless he could run the table, he was going to have to count on Panhead baiting him for at least another game. Carl decided to help him along.

"This is where I start making a dent in that roll of yours," Carl said with a wink. He slapped his money down beside Panhead's and made his break.

"Not bad," Panhead said as the 4 ball went in.

Carl let loose a silent sigh. He was a fifty-fifty breaker at best, and he'd made the lucky fifty this time. He followed it up by dropping 1 through 6 on a series of—if he had to admit it—brilliant shots. But then he left himself a bad lie and missed the 7.

"Nice run," Panhead said as he settled in to set up his own shot.

Had Carl played too well? A hustler who thinks he might lose will take what he can get and be done with it. Three balls to go was easy enough to mop up, and Carl would be back to bus fare. Hotel money was riding on this game, and hearse money on the next. This was the one he wanted to win.

"Yeah, until I gave it away," Carl said. "Jesus, I can't buy a damn bank shot. Maybe this isn't my night, after all."

Panhead chuckled as he aimed, squinting with one eye. "Maybe it ain't." He took a shot and slammed home the 7. Then the 8. Then... he missed the 9. It rattled around a corner pocket and bounced out.

"Ouch," Carl said. "Tough break. I'll give you a rematch." His own shot was a gimme, and he made it. He was up sixty dollars.

"Make it eighty," Panhead said. "Lemme have a chance to make my money back."

"Make it a hundred," Carl replied with a grin. "I've got a bookie to pay off. Just lemme go grab a smoke." Carl had never smoked in his life. He'd grown up shipboard, where putting an unnecessary load on the life-support systems was frowned upon. Some of the luxury cruise ships let you smoke, but the navy and Chuck Ramsey didn't put up with that shit in their air filtration.

He strutted over to his jacket and took it from its peg on the wall. He made a show of looking through the pockets. "Hey, can I bum a cigarette?" he asked the pool hall at large. One of Panhead's biker friends obliged, offering him a cigarette from a bland red-and-white package. Carl scooped a book of matches off the bar and headed for the front door. "Back in five."

Once outside and with the door closed behind him, Carl abandoned "cool" in favor of haste. He shrugged on his jacket and headed for the first car in the lot. It was a vintage replica petrol-burner, powder blue with white side panels and fins on the back. It was unlocked, because this was supposed to be a utopian paradise where people didn't steal cars.

But they still had keys for the ignition. Fucking retroverts and their nonsensical nostalgia. Either they should have locked the damn cars or done away with keyed ignitions. He checked above the visor, under the seat, and in the glove box, but the owner hadn't left his keys anywhere in the vehicle.

The logical, rational part of Carl's mind told him to try the next car. Someone around here was bound to have been trusting enough to leave keys in the ignition for him. A passing wish for the assistance of a certain laaku mechanic flashed in his mind. Hot-wiring looked so easy on an old flatvid, but he hadn't the foggiest idea how to do it. But both the rational and wishful parts of Carl made way for the juggernaut that was the flamboyant option.

A row of motorcycles parked in formation at the side of the lot. One caught his eye. Laid back. Extended front wheel. Giant handlebars. Engine half the size of the vehicle. Those things didn't usually have keys, as far as he could remember. Checking over his shoulder to make sure no one was exiting the bar, he headed over and took a closer look at his new ride.

It was no Squall. It wouldn't get him airborne without a ramp. If he needed it to, he could outrun most four-wheeled vehicles native to the time period. Straddling the seat, he grabbed the handlebars and walked the chopper back. It was heavier than it looked, but in neutral he could get it moving with just his feet.

The controls were a mystery. No flatvid he'd ever watched had given a close-up on the console to show the startup sequence. He flipped switches and pulled levers until one made noise. It gave a pathetic petrol-motor cough and went silent. The two parts of the controls Carl was certain of were the right grip and the kickstarter. Hoping that he'd stumbled onto the missing link, he hit the starter switch, twisted the grip, and put his weight down on the kick start lever. The bike made a variety of unpleasant noises in protest.

"Hey!"

That was Carl's key to hurry. One of Panhead's biker friends had poked his head out to investigate. It was double-down or buy time.

"This thing got a lighter?" Carl asked. He stomped down on the kickstart lever again, hoping that maybe the simplest solution was the best. Nothing.

Bikers poured out of Sharky's. Carl gave one final attempt at the kickstart lever with the grip twisted, but that didn't work either.

"Look fellas, there's no need to—"

But they weren't in the mood for listening. Carl was lifted from the motorcycle's seat. He felt fists slam into his kidneys and his gut, blinding him in pain and robbing him of his breath. He fell to the asphalt, gasping. If he could convince them of...well *anything*, it might have been possible to save himself from getting killed and left for dead in a ditch. But he couldn't get out more than a croak and not even an articulate one at that.

They started in with the boots, pummeling him in the legs, stomping on his back. One caught him in the head, and he didn't notice the rest.

The chaise drifted down and settled onto the stone floor. Mort leaned on his mop and gave a satisfied sigh. "Done. Or at least done enough. We should freshen up so it doesn't look like we spent the day as housemaids."

Esper dropper her feather duster and rolled down the sleeves of her dress. "Finally. You know, I kept my mouth shut all day, wondering if this was another sort of test. But I have to ask: why didn't you just use magic to clean? I mean, you lifted the furniture out of the way, why not march the whole parade route?"

"I have a reputation to maintain," Mort replied, collapsing onto the chaise he had just returned to the floor.

"I would have thought *not* cleaning would have suited you better. Besides, it's just you and me here."

"In one respect, perhaps, but the universe is always watching," Mort said. "It has an image of me as an agent of destruction and chaos, a tinkerer with gravity and astral navigation. My arguments often run afoul of cleanliness and order, and if I started wheedling for tidied shelves and mildew-free floors, I'd be making a hypocrite of myself. Not worth it."

"You mean..."

"One of two things might have happened," Mort said. "No, make that three. The third would be no harm at all, which I suppose is a legitimate outcome. As for the other two scenarios, I could have altered the universe's opinion of me in ways that would reduce my effectiveness in making my more typical arguments. I also could have accidentally tapped into my more destructive reputation and had some sort of cleaning cataclysm."

"Like the fable of the Sorcerer's Apprentice?" Esper asked.

"You've been watching those ancient flatvids, huh?" Mort

asked, and Esper nodded in reply. "Well, there's truth in that one. Not the musical, dancing mops, mind you, but the magic gone over the rancher's fence. A stampede, as it were. I might have unleashed a tornado trying to dust, or a tsunami washing the floors. Best to just roll up our sleeves and do a bit of light peasant work."

"Those peasants of yours might have helped if you paid them," Esper said.

"They live on my land!" Mort objected. "Rent free for years. You'd think proper caretaking services wouldn't be too much to ask in return."

A bell sounded from the entry hall. "That's either an angry mob, or your lady friend is here," Esper said.

Mort harrumphed. "Looks like break time is over." He paused at a freshly washed mirror before heading out to answer the door.

Esper followed a few paces behind. She didn't care much what she looked like. If Keesha Bell decided that Esper looked like she'd been doing chores all day, so be it. Sometimes the truth was better than a veneer of propriety.

Mort opened the ornate, wood-carved door himself. Standing outside was a woman with dark skin and white hair. Her features looked middle-aged, but her past history with Mort and her hair color painted a different portrait. Esper shouldn't have been one to judge, since Tanny said she looked more like sixteen than twenty-four.

"Mordecai, I hardly believed I'd see you again after you dodged me on Champlain," Keesha said. She smiled as Mort took her hand and kissed it.

"I had business," Mort said. "I'm not always at liberty to pay social calls."

"No, only when it serves you," Keesha said with a sigh,

stepping into the entry hall. A prim, tidy, quiet gentleman followed her inside. "I trust this is Miss Richelieu."

"Esper, ma'am," Esper said with a curtsy. Given her attire and surroundings, it seemed appropriate, even though she'd only seen curtsies on holovid.

Keesha looked her up and down, then gave a sly glance over at Mort. Esper felt her cheeks burning. Why did everyone seem to hint that she was having some sort of relationship with Mort? "I assume you've been told why I'm here?"

"You know about the woman who took Kubu captive," Esper said. She figured that if Keesha didn't want her assistant to know, she'd have kept her voice down.

Keesha frowned at Mort.

"I thought it would be a nice surprise," Mort said.

"What do you mean?" Esper asked. "What surprise?"

"In due time, child," Keesha said. "First, Mordecai and I have some business of our own. Be a dear and show Hobson someplace he can rest his feet for a few hours."

"What'll you be—" Esper clipped off the end of her own question as Mort took Keesha by the hand and led her from the room. The grins on their faces told her more than she wanted to know. She turned to Hobson. "I guess we're on our own for the foreseeable future."

"It would appear so," Hobson replied.

They retired to the freshly cleaned sitting room. Even with the windows thrown wide open, the room still clung to a scent of must and mildew. Hobson was the perfect guest though, and didn't even comment about it. He sat stiff and tall without giving a hint of discomfort; he was totally at ease keeping a rigid posture. He exuded butlerism.

Once Esper broke the ice, however, he became a charming and informative conversationalist. She wormed free the stories about Mort and Keesha's past relationship. She'd been friends with Mort's wife ages ago and had taken him in for a summer between Mort's tenure with Chuck Ramsey's ship and Carl purchasing the *Mobius*. Despite her wheedling, Esper couldn't get Hobson to admit that their relationship had been anything but platonic. Esper found that hard to swallow.

The conversation redirected toward Esper after a while and the series of misadventures that had landed her a bunk on Carl's ship. It was a better story than she'd imagined as she started telling it. Her early life had become too easy to sum up in a few words that she had forgotten how much the details had shaped her. Once she got to her life aboard the *Mobius*, she became a little more cautious. She didn't know Hobson, and the sort of things she'd done as a member of the crew were a great fountain of blackmail material. Still, with careful editing and omissions, she gave Hobson the idea of their adventures.

"So I guess I have your boss to thank for finding Kubu in the first place," Esper said. "If it wasn't for her sending us off, we'd never have found that crazy zoo or helped all those people. Honestly, I think I did more for the greater good of sentient-kind that day than I did in my years teaching math as a priestess in a church-run school."

"Did you always have a fondness for mathematics?" Hobson asked.

"Fondness? Goodness no! I was always *good* at it though. Part of learning humility is knowing when to do what needs to be done, instead of what you like doing."

"And is that why Mordecai has been teaching you magic?" Hobson asked. "Because you have an affinity for it?"

Esper looked down at her hands. "That's not it. I mean... well, you know. Not everyone *can*. And I can't always resist, especially when someone's in trouble and I think I can help. It's just... well, it hasn't always worked out, and Mort's been trying to teach me the big picture. He says if I know what I'm doing, I won't do it by accident."

"So you'd be a wizard either way, but Mordecai is teaching you the right way?"

"Something like that, I suppose," Esper said. Hobson nodded almost imperceptibly. Was he judging her? "What's it to you why Mort is teaching me?"

Hobson offered a wan smile. "My apologies. Miss Bell insisted on knowing."

"She's the jealous type?" Esper asked.

"She is merely careful of her associates."

"Not careful enough, if she still comes to see Mort," Esper replied. She felt an instant pang of guilt at the hurt look she received in reply.

"You have no idea how deep those two are twined."

"Then tell me," Esper said. It wasn't fair dangling juicy gossip then clamming up immediately.

"Ask one or the other of them," Hobson said. "I have no right to speculate, and much of what I would say is indeed mere speculation."

Esper steered the conversation back to small talk until Mort and Keesha came back. The giddy energy had passed, but both looked in fine spirits. Keesha's hair was too short to muss, but Mort's looked none the worse for their absence. Everyone's clothes were on properly. Maybe she had the wrong idea about what had been going on elsewhere in the keep.

"Stand up, child," Keesha said. It was a command, firm, but not overbearing. Somehow it didn't seem like the time to argue that she was a grown woman and didn't have to do any such thing. Esper stood.

She looked to Mort. "So you found out where—"

Mort held up a hand, nodding. "Yes. Later."

Keesha produced a sphere of dark, polished glass and held it out. "Esper Theresa Richelieu," Keesha said. "Repeat after me. I solemnly swear..." The sphere lit with a soft glow from within.

Esper looked to Mort, wide eyed. But Mort gave her a wink and a nod. What was that supposed to mean? Those words weren't the sort you just echoed lightly. But Mort made a hurry-up motion with his hand, keeping silent and raising his eyebrows in obvious exasperation.

Esper took a deep breath. "I solemnly swear."

"That I will uphold the laws and traditions of the Convocation... That I will heed my master in my studies, but never abdicate my own free will... That I will take responsibility for the power I possess and the powers I shall learn... That I will keep secret the old ways, and not be drawn by the lures of science... That I will not misuse my powers, or allow them to fester unused... That I will seek wisdom, knowledge, and control of the forces I might harness... That I will act in the best interests of the Convocation, humankind, and the magic-capable species of the cosmos... That I will do so of my own free will and best interest in exchange for inclusion into the most ancient and noble institution of humankind."

Esper parroted along in a daze. She was under no spell or compulsion, but she didn't know if she could have stopped herself from being carried along. She was a joiner. She hadn't realized just how isolated she'd felt until she recited those words. Cut off from friends and family of her own choice, she joined the One Church. Disillusioned with the church, she'd taken up with the *Mobius* crew. Having faked her own death, she couldn't even walk the streets—or pedestrian tubes—of a modern city. Now, the Convocation was taking her in.

Keesha Bell nodded as Esper finished, then put a finger to her lips. "I, Keesha Bell, do swear this oath was taken under neither threat nor geas. I shall uphold my duties as master and take Esper Theresa Richelieu as my apprentice." The glow faded.

Esper looked from Keesha to Mort and back, her mouth agape.

"Hold your horses," Mort said. "Before that brain of yours crawls out, it's a formality."

"Mordecai can't take an apprentice officially," Keesha said. "But aside from records in an old ledger in some dusty building on Earth, you'll be *his* apprentice, not mine. It's not as the Convocation sends inspectors out to the Champlain System to check on apprentices' well-being."

"We'll get you a medallion from a silversmith somewhere around here," Mort said. Under his breath, he added, "Not from that ingrate down in *my* village though."

"Farewell, Mordecai," Keesha said, turning to leave. Hobson hastened to get past her to see to the doors. "We should do this more often."

"We should," Mort agreed.

Esper kept silent until the two guests had disappeared behind the closed front door. "How can you just let her go? She was only here a couple hours. I mean... you can... you know."

Mort chuckled. "We got a lot of use out of those two hours."

Esper narrowed her eyes. "Just what is it between the two of you?"

To her surprise, Mort let out a wistful sigh and answered. "We spent a lifetime together, one summer long ago."

Tanny paced the common room while Roddy sat back and watched as if she were some sort of holovid. She needed to think, to bounce ideas off someone, and the laaku wasn't helping. Everyone on the *Mobius* had gotten used to the fact that Roddy was almost constantly drunk—a little drunk. Right now his veins carried more beer than blood.

Agheli and his techs had been gone for more than an hour. Despite it being the middle of the night, neither of them had been able to sleep. "This is going to be bad," Tanny said. "We can't comm Rhiannon because she doesn't have a modern comm at home, and if we try the local wire-lines, I'm sure they're bugged."

Roddy giggled. "Liar, liar, bugs in the wire."

"We've got no way to get a hold of Mort, Esper, or Mriy," she continued, ignoring Roddy as much as she could. "And who the hell knows where Carl ran off with his toy Squall. I mean, turning off anything that broadcasts was great for sneaking away, but now *we* can't find it either."

Roddy wagged a finger. "You. You, you, you. You... not beer enough." He patted the couch cushion beside him.

Tanny rubbed her eyes. "You're not helping."

"I'm not... jail sobering," he replied. "Getting all the drunk I am while I can."

"If you were sober, think you could fix the star-drive?" Tanny asked. "At least then we wouldn't be sitting ducks if they come for us."

Roddy opened his mouth, aghast. "Don't sit on ducks! Cute and little. You'd hurt 'em."

"The star-drive, Roddy. The star-drive. Can you put it back together?"

"Whadda I look like to you?" Roddy asked. "A wizard? Two wizards? Three? I'm zero wizards, big girl. You know... with more fur on you—"

"Forget it," Tanny said, cutting him off before she found out what Roddy was thinking about, picturing her with fur. "We can't just disappear on this world, and we can't run. We're going to have to hang tight and hope everyone else's stories cross-check. Or at least hope everyone has the sense to come back to the *Mobius* before they come to round us up."

Tanny paused, expecting Roddy to respond with some sloppy-drunk, unhelpful reply, but none was forthcoming. The laaku mechanic had slumped over onto his side, beer dripping onto the couch from a half-empty can held limp in one foot.

"Roddy?" she asked. It was no time to be falling asleep. They had no plan, and they needed one. "Wake up!" She shook him by the shoulder, but he was unresponsive. A quick shot of panic quickened her heart. Had he finally drunk himself to death? She'd warned him of that possibility enough times for it to spring readily to mind. She checked his wrist for a pulse—nothing. She was no medic. Maybe she'd done it wrong. She checked his neck, but the fur made it too hard to tell if the heartbeat she felt was Roddy's or her own. She unbuttoned the top of Roddy's coveralls and put an ear to his chest.

Before she was certain she'd heard a beating heart, a hand flopped down on her back. "Hey, baby," Roddy slurred. "You like what... see?" He began to snore.

Fuming, Tanny disentangled herself from the comatose laaku. Lifting him by the collar of his unbuttoned coveralls, she dragged him to the shower, hit the start sequence, and closed him inside.

The sound of falling water came a split second before a groggy moan. "Wha—? Where? Why's it raining in here?"

"I'm putting on coffee," Tanny called through the door. "If that doesn't work, you're trying one of my Adrenophiline pills.

You give me the least bit of shit about it, I flush the ship's beer reserves. Capisce?"

Another moan emanated from the shower. "I'm in no shape for mixing languages."

"It means—"

"I'm drunk, not stupid," Roddy shouted feebly through the door. "Gimme a minute, *two* of those damn pills of yours, and find me something dry from my room."

"One pill," Tanny replied. One was probably an unsafe dosage for a laaku half her size. "But you've got a deal."

She put a pot of coffee on anyway, as she headed to round up a change of clothes and an Adrenophiline pill. Even if Roddy didn't want it, *she* needed all the help she could get. They were stranded on a self-imposed primitive world with the crew scattered. They couldn't take the *Mobius* out of the system without Mort or at least someone to repair the stardrive. And worst of all, there was a laaku fact sifter who was doing a dogged job of digging into the crew's recent history.

Two hundred fifty thousand terras. If Carl had played that race straight, he'd have walked away with all of it. Instead, they had a Squall they couldn't sell, a blackmailer who forced Carl to fake his death, and a branch of the Phabian government investigating the crash that supposedly killed him. The Phabian Investigative Service wasn't known for rash judgments, mistakes, or corruption. The noose was closing, and they were running out of time to slip it. Tanny seemed to be the only one aware of that.

Mort had cooked.

They sat at either end of a servants' table in the kitchens, paddling at the watery broth, salty enough to pass for seawater. They had both given up eating the soup, having dredged forth the bits of chicken and carrot that had been edible. Esper's bread rested beside her bowl, one bite gone from the stale half-loaf.

"Just out with it," Mort snapped, breaking a long silence.

Esper flinched. "Sorry. Maybe we should have just gone down to the village for dinner."

Mort squinted one eye. Apparently she had puzzled him somehow. He spared a glance down at his own bowl, then tossed it over his shoulder. "Not that. The soup is rubbish and we both know it. No point kicking the carcass. No, that question you've been gnawing at since Keesha left. I'd been waiting to see how long you'd avoid asking, but I came to the decision that you were going to bury it in that little cloister you've got in your head. I'm not the easily offended sort, you know."

"If you know the question, then what's the answer?" Esper asked, turning his assumptions back on him. If Mort wanted to play the I-know-what-you-know game, she'd play it right back. She wasn't going to venture forth another errant opinion and prompt another bowl-throwing incident.

Mort shook his head. "Ask."

Esper sighed. "Fine. What did you mean that you spent a lifetime together with Keesha Bell one summer?"

The grin that lit Mort's face told her before he said a word that she'd picked correctly. "Aha! I'll show you."

Mort dragged his chair around Esper's side of the table, then turned the two chairs to face each other. Despite Mort's hands on the chair, she knew he'd used magic to accomplish the actual moving. She wasn't *that* heavy, but she and the chair combined ought to have been more than a spindly old wizard could just slide around at ease.

"What are you doing?" she asked.

"Showing you."

"You rearranged kitchen furniture?" Esper asked. "You practiced magicking chairs around? You spent the summer avoiding a lifetime's worth of inedible soup?"

Her last guess prompted a chuckle from Mort. "Well, the showing part comes up in just a bit." He sat down facing her and leaned close. Esper stiffened. She wasn't sure what he was up to, but her personal space was shrinking rapidly. Mort slipped a hand behind her neck and pulled gently until their foreheads touched. "Now just relax..."

Esper jerked awake as if from a waking dream, the sort where your mind had wandered off in the middle of some boring task and returned with sudden alertness. She wasn't in the kitchen of Thunderglade Keep any longer. The dank, un-lived-in smell was gone, replaced by the wafting scent of spring flowers carried on a warm breeze. She was standing on a stone balcony, looking out over a vast stretch of green meadows that ended in a forest kilometers away.

She took a step toward the railing and stumbled, catching her balance before she fell. Her flat-soled slippers were gone, replaced by tall, heeled shoes. Glancing down at herself, her outfit had undergone a complete transformation. Her noblewoman's dress had been replaced by a gown fit for a princess, pale pink and flowered in elaborate white embroidery and laced at the cuffs and around the neckline. It was more comfortable and lighter than the other dress, tailored to fit perfectly and less confining around the neck. Her fingers bore thin silver rings set with jewels, and a necklace of pearls hugged her throat. She could only imagine that the earrings matched, feeling them dangle as she looked around.

A chuckle from behind made her twist around, nearly losing her balance once again. "What do you think?"

Mort stood at the doorway to the balcony, dressed as he had been in the kitchen, though a bit cleaner. The gray was gone from his hair, and the wrinkles smoothed from his face. He looked twenty years younger.

"What happened?" Esper asked. "Where are we?"

Mort swept a hand toward the countryside. "I call it... Mortania."

"What happened to Thunderglade?"

Mort scoffed. "What? That old hovel? Nothing. We're still there."

Esper glanced over the balcony railing, scanning left and right. "I don't see any sign of the village. You weren't exactly located on the edge of town."

"Oh, this isn't a regular old place," Mort said.

The wizard raised his arms and a thunderhead rallied to his call. Within seconds, the sun had been obscured behind black storm clouds. Lightning leapt from the heavens, striking the tower high over their heads. Esper ducked behind Mort as the thunder hammered through her.

"Mort?" she shouted. "Whatever you're doing, stop it!"

A bestial shriek from the tower above drove aside all worries over the thunderstorm. It was unlike anything Esper had ever heard—or was it? It did bear an uncanny resemblance to a holovid she and Mort had watched recently, except this was real. That meant it couldn't be a... dragon?

The flapping of leathery wings forced her eyes to turn skyward. Above was a creature of myth and nightmare. Black scales. Eyes like a snake. Claws and fangs fit to tear human flesh to ribbons.

"Mort, do something!"

"Kythrast, heel!" Mort shouted. The dragon descended, its flapping wings raising a storm that whipped Esper's hair and the fabric of her dress. Kythrast stopped with his nose level with the balcony. Mort put a foot onto the stone railing and extended a hand to Esper. "Welcome aboard."

"Are you crazy? That's a *dragon*."

"Of course it's a dragon," Mort said. "This is my imagination. I created it."

The phone rang. Rhiannon set down her morning coffee and picked up the receiver. "Ramsey residence. Rhiannon speaking."

The voice on the other end of the line came in clarion clear, which should have been her first clue that this was an unusual call. Transit distance always made period-authentic calls scratchy and audibly distorted. "Miss Ramsey, this is Fact Sifter Agheli of the Phabian Investigative Service. Do you have a moment to answer a few questions?"

It was a loaded question. There was no "no" option. Trying would only get her the "afraid I have to insist" line. So predictable. But this was PIS, the opening act for Laaku Bureaucrat and the Predictables. "Sure. Just coffeeing up for the day. What can I do you for?" She cradled the receiver against her shoulder as she topped off her cup and added sugars. This could be a long call.

"Thank you for your cooperation," Agheli replied. With a click, the line went dead. Seconds later, there was a knock at the door.

"Shit," Rhiannon muttered. The bastard had called from

just outside the house. Probably an induction tap into the phone grid, modern tech slipping into the archaic system like a wolf among terriers.

Rhiannon paused a moment to listen. The sound of running water from upstairs let her know that Lloyd was still in the shower. There was no time to get stories straight, or to prepare him for their unexpected guests. She hurried to the door before Agheli became suspicious.

A laaku in a snappy PIS uniform smiled up at her from her doorstep. "Thank you for your accommodation. I hope to keep this brief." Agheli stepped into the house without asking for an explicit invitation. He was alone. It was always tempting to look down at a 1.3-meter tall fuzzball and think she could just knock his head in. He was the size of a six-year-old. But even if it *wasn't* for the fact that he was probably quite a bit stronger than her, Rhiannon couldn't imagine getting away with it. She'd be on the run, and unlike her brother, no one would think she was dead.

Her purse sat on a side table. Rummaging through it, she found a pack of cigarettes and a lighter. "Mind if I smoke?" she asked belatedly, taking her first puff.

Agheli turned his head slightly aside and blocked his nose and mouth with the back of one hand. "I do recall local ordinances allowing tobacco exhaust discharge. Proceed."

"You got questions," Rhiannon said, and let out a long, smoky breath in Agheli's direction. "Shoot. You already know I visited Tanny and Roddy last night, so you know I know what this is about."

"Your citizen file lists your occupation as entertainer," Agheli said.

"You got it, daddy-O," Rhiannon said, half leaning, half sitting on the arm of a chair. "I don't dance. I don't play. I just sing it." The cigarette was already starting to relax her, and this

Agheli square didn't have the scanners with him to know it wasn't tobacco.

"Can you account for your whereabouts during the months of December of last year, specifically the time from December 6 through the present?" Agheli asked, glancing to his datapad for reference.

Rhiannon let her head loll back and blew a smoke ring—or at least made an attempt. "Well, right now I'm here. And before that, I got myself to some gigs. But I haven't been off-world since last summer. So if you're trying to pin Carl's death on me... flake off."

Agheli furrowed his brow and referenced his datapad. It beeped and blooped. Rhiannon could only imagine the mental gymnastics he was doing to make sure he knew what she'd said. Laaku might grow up learning the language, but that didn't mean they knew the lingo. At least not New Cali lingo.

Agheli cleared his throat. "Well, no. We don't *suspect* anything. Suspicion is not part of my job. I am a fact sifter. My findings will be passed on to other branches of Investigative Services. Now, can you please provide independent verification of your whereabouts for the time in question?"

"Talk to my agent," Rhiannon replied. "You wanna ask me a question, lay it on me. But don't hassle me about paperwork. You dig?"

Agheli's frown deepened, but he didn't resort to his datapad. "Had your brother contacted you prior to his demise?"

"Fucker only ever commed if he needed scratch." When this didn't seem to satisfy the laaku flatfoot—could laaku even *be* flatfooted?—she added, "No."

"Did he ever exhibit self-destructive behavior before, during, or after his service in Earth Navy?"

Laughter bubbled in Rhiannon until it burst forth, unable to remain bottled up. "Carl? Off himself? Noodle it out, man.

My brother's had people shooting at him, like, half his life. I mean, like his whole situation is self-destructive, but his whole bag is doing his own thing. Why've you gotta go making it a federal case?"

"I'm not sure you've answered my question," Agheli replied. "And this isn't a federal case; this is being handled at the system level, under Central Phabian jurisdiction."

"Then you don't have any authority here," Lloyd said, stepping into the room in an undershirt and slacks, barefoot and with his hair still wet from the shower. "This is Peractorum. We're under ARGO jurisdiction, or Earth's. If you're acting as an agent of Central Phabian authority, I'm going to have to advise Rhiannon to seek legal counsel before continuing this debriefing."

Rhiannon tugged Lloyd over and kissed him. It was incredibly sexy when he acted all lawyerish at someone—besides her. "Thanks, Pumpkin. He was really starting to harsh my... tobacco." She hid a giggle behind pursed lips.

He pointed to the cigarette dangling from her fingers. "Why don't you finish that in the back yard? I need to have a few words with the fact sifter here."

"Right on," Rhiannon said. "You tell him, baby."

She waggled her fingers at Agheli in a parting wave and headed out back. It was morning, and the dewy grass tickled her feet. All those little droplets...

By the time she'd finished smoking, she'd lost count of the tiny worlds of water, each possibly having its own little planets and suns of their very own. She was a starship, flying from one to the next. Lloyd's voice snapped her out of her daydream.

"All clear," he said. "Come say goodbye to our guest."

Rhiannon stepped past Lloyd as he held the screen door for her. Hips swaying, she thought of all the things she could do to keep Lloyd at home to reward him for being her hero, getting rid of the little laaku narc—who was still there in the family room.

Agheli stood as Rhiannon entered the room. "I believe I have all the information I need. I will be returning to my ship. I will have no further questions."

Rhiannon gave him a goofy smile. "Aw, shucks. Could've saved you the ride, man. Told ya that, like, yesterday."

Agheli stiffened, eyes wide. "I believe I have all the information I need. I will be returning to my ship. I will have no further questions."

Rhiannon looked to Lloyd. "This guy's got a broken record."

Agheli didn't resist as Lloyd ushered him first to the door, then through it. "It was nice meeting you," he said. As soon as the door was closed, he scowled. "And *you*. What were you thinking giving an official deposition blitzed out of your skull?"

Rhiannon closed her eyes and waved her hands. "Shh. I got it figured out. Carl always said he could beat the truth scanners, and I think he must be stoned *all the time*. It would, like, explain *everything*."

"That's a myth," Lloyd replied. "Certain drugs can defeat a majority of tests, as can wizards and people with certain cybernetic enhancements. But I think your brother is just full of shit."

Carl regained consciousness. Given the circumstances he last remembered, that was always a bonus. Those bikers could have killed him without half trying. Fortunately they'd only wanted to send a message, and Carl had gotten it loud and clear: no more stealing motorcycles until he learned how to drive one.

Taking stock of his surroundings, Carl found himself in an all-white room that smelled of antiseptics. He was lying in bed under starched linens, where he wore nothing but a cotton smock. The clothes he had worn the night before—or however long ago his encounter at Sharky's had been—were folded and piled on the seat of a vinyl-cushioned armchair in the corner. His bedside table was barren except for a glass filled with water. Thirsty, he gave it a sniff to be sure it *was* just water and drank.

No sooner had he set the glass down when someone entered. She was dressed all in pristine white, blending perfectly with the decor. Her short-sleeved uniform top was covered by an apron-like dress that swished around her ankles as she walked. There was some sort of bonnet or hat on her head that didn't seem to serve any clear purpose. She wasn't young or particularly old.

"Good to see you awake," she said. "I'm Dr. Singh. You're in recovery room 2A at St. Luke Medical Center in Anaheim."

"Prime?" Carl asked.

Dr. Singh smiled. "You're not on Earth. This is still Peractorum, still New Cali. How are you feeling?"

Carl blinked. He hadn't given the matter much thought. He wasn't in pain, which should have been surprising. It was possible his veins were swimming in painkillers—the twentieth century's stock answer for everything they couldn't fix—but he felt lucid. Lucid enough to remember how he'd gotten himself beaten up in the first place.

He put a hand to his face, covering one eye and grimacing. "I... I think I'm OK. I don't remember how I got here."'

"You don't have memory loss," Dr. Singh replied. "You were admitted with six fractured ribs, a fractured jaw, two missing teeth with damage to four others, severe concussion, cranial hemorrhaging, and various lacerations and contusions. But despite the period ambiance, this is a Class 2 medical facility. You're fine... whoever you are."

Scowling at Dr. Singh, Carl felt around the inside of his mouth with his tongue. "Which two aren't mine?" He didn't feel any missing teeth, or anything unusual about the ones he had.

"You'd never tell without a med scan," Dr. Singh replied. "However, the subject of your identity is something the authorities are going to want to discuss with you. Normally I'd assume someone without a positive DNA match was born on-world and never left. Paperwork is sloppy around here, especially in some of the old-tech colonies. But you... you've got starship-grade impurities in your bloodstream. We did a blood scrub, but you've clearly spent a lot of time breathing reprocessed air with a sub-par antibacterial and anti-viral agents added. And the DNA match we *did* make... it was to a dead man."

It came out as a reflex. "I can explain—"

"That you *are* or *are not* Bradley Carlin Ramsey?" Dr. Singh asked. Carl knew he'd given himself away when he flinched. He hadn't expected her to be so bold in confronting him. In Carl's experience, that was usually the sort of thing that got deferred to gentlemen with stun batons.

"Would you even believe me if I said I wasn't?" Carl asked.

"Depends. You've got blue hair, which shouldn't be possible given your follicle biochemistry. It's consistent with your bio and the promos from that holovid racing series."

Carl was willing to work with that. He even had a story in place, much as he'd hoped to hold onto it longer. "I've been cloned."

Dr. Singh folded her arms and fixed Carl with a stern look.

"Honest to God," Carl replied, holding up a hand to swear an oath. "I'm not making this up. There is a company out there that—"

"Illegal human cloning," Dr. Singh said. "It's a quiet blight in the medical community. But they don't go around cloning... how can I put this delicately—"

"Expert pilots?" Carl suggested. "Ex-Navy heroes?"

"Sub-optimal specimens," Dr. Singh said, offering a brief, weak smile. "Most rescued clones end up enlisting in the marines, or going into advanced scientific fields. Minds and bodies at the zenith of human potential. I've even heard of them attempting to clone wizards, but nothing that bore fruit. Please don't take this the wrong way, but you're just not the type." With a shrug she turned to leave.

Carl lunged and grabbed the hem of her dress. "Please! Do me a favor, before you go turning me over to anyone," Carl said. "Check the news feeds of the investigation. They know something's up, but haven't figured it out yet."

"Phabian has the best forensics facilities outside of Earth," Dr. Singh replied, yanking the hem of her dress free. "I'm sure they could tell cloned tissue from naturally grown. *You* certainly aren't cloned."

"I might be," Carl said. "It was Harmony Bay that did it. If anyone could fool Phabian's snoops, it's them. I don't know if it's the dead guy or me that was the original." Let her stew on that one.

Dr. Singh stared down at Carl, muscles tight in her jaw. "You stay put. I'll check out your story and schedule you for more scans. If you sneak out, I'll call the police."

"Will there be sponge baths if I stay?" Carl asked with a twinkle in his eye. Dr. Singh wasn't his type, exactly, but it never hurt to try the angle.

Dr. Singh stepped over to Carl's bedside as he settled back

after his lunge. She leaned down and put her lips by his ear. "Just in case you're thinking of pulling a fast one..."

There was a sharp pressure against Carl's shoulder and a quick hiss. A warm sensation spread from the spot, dispersing through his bloodstream. As Carl fought to keep his eyes open, he saw Dr. Singh slip a pencil-sized metal cylinder into her pocket. "You..." it was as far as he got before his voice failed him.

"Just sedated you," Dr. Singh finished for him. "If your story is true, you've got nothing to worry about."

Carl drifted into drug-induced sleep quite worried.

Tanny sat on the common room couch, elbows on knees, chin on clasped hands, feet tapping. A late night's fruitless planning had led her and Roddy to conclude that their best bet was sitting tight. If everyone's stories held together, Phabian Investigative Service would have no reason to suspect any involvement by the *Mobius* crew. The ship's alibi was unassailable. The crew had all made sure to be seen off-world well out of range of any normal ship's best astral drive. If the authorities were suspicious of Carl's apparent death—and by news-feed accounts, they were—then fine. If they thought Tanny and the rest of them were covering something up—also fine. It wasn't as if they hadn't always acted like they were trying to slip something past the watchdog. Just so long as nobody could put those two suspicions together with even circumstantial evidence, it would blow over.

Sitting tight. Tanny hated it.

There were times in the service when her detachment had been forced to wait for circumstances beyond their control to determine their fate. On Geronn Minor, her transport had been grounded while Earth Navy and an Eyndar battle group duked it out in orbit to see whose ground forces would get obliterated by the victor. After the battle of Tynar IV, the *Supremacy* had been left adrift with minimal life support for three days. An entire fleet carrier filled with sailors and marines, each secretly wondering whether killing some crew mates would mean fewer lungs sucking up the air. This time, only a prison term hung over her head, but that was scant comfort.

The groan of someone forcing open the cargo ramp hydraulics made her stiffen. Her first instinct told her someone was breaking into the ship. Her second was that Mort was the one who found it easier to force the mechanism than figure out the ramp controls. She rushed to the door leading down to the cargo bay, stopping at the last second to loosen her blaster pistol in its holster at her thigh. In case it wasn't Mort.

"Hullo up there," Mort's voice echoed, muffled through the door. Tanny opened it with a sigh of relief. "Ah, there you are. Thought maybe everyone had gone out for Chinese."

"No, still just Mriy," Tanny replied. Mriy had enrolled in a course at one of the Shaolin temples in the Celestial Empire. It was a tourist trap with a sketchy VacationBlab rating, but it was how the azrin wanted to spend her time planetside. The thought of a clawed, 120-kilo felid with mystical martial arts training gave her the shudders. But it wasn't like she'd get much more than a guided tour in the few days she'd be there.

Esper was with Mort. She looked up and made eye contact with Tanny briefly, but didn't say anything. She followed Mort into the ship, not bothering with the controls to raise the ramp behind them. Something about the way her gaze wandered the cargo bay seemed off, like she was lost or looking for something.

"You find out what we needed to get Kubu back?" Tanny asked. She could have a talk with Esper later. Right now, she had a dog to get back. Or a son. Or some weird hybrid of the two. Kubu didn't fit into a neat checkbox.

Mort patted a leather pouch tied to his belt. "Crystal thingamajiggy's got it all, she said. I got the low-down on the down-low, so to speak though. That laaku witch has him. She's been up to shit like this for years, 'rescuing' animals and sentients who've been treated like them. Zoos, labs, private collectors. If they don't have good lawyers, she claims custody and takes possession. Nice scam if you can pull it off. The lawyers might even be cheaper than buying exotics." By the time Mort finished talking, he'd reached the top of the stairs.

"But what about a rescue plan?" Tanny asked. "Security systems? Guards? Architectural schematics?"

"Keesha assured me everything we need is on this," Mort said, pressing a datacrystal into Tanny's hand. He stepped around her and into the common room, heading straight for the fridge. "Now what've we got to eat around here?"

Tanny caught Esper by the arm as she tried to follow Mort. "Are you all right? You look like hell." Esper seemed to be in a daze. Her fairy-princess medieval getup was stained with sweat and dirty from the knees to the hem. It looked like she hadn't slept in days.

"It's... just a little strange being back," Esper replied. She shrugged free of Tanny's grip.

"You were gone what... two days?" Tanny asked. It wasn't as if she'd really been away. Then again, maybe mentally she had. Tanny lowered her voice as Mort settled onto the couch with a bag of insta-pop popcorn and a beer. "Did Mort... do anything to you? If you need to talk, you can trust me."

The "what would we do if Mort went nuts on us" plan had always been a little iffy. Quietly, on the side, she and Carl had figured out how to handle it if any of the crew ever turned on them. For some, the precautions were trivial. When they first took on Mriy, it had involved taking on some additional blaster pistols with a human-lethal stun setting, just in case. But Mort they had no plan for. Hope, luck, and Mort's conscience were their only protections.

But Esper's snorting, suppressed laugh put Tanny's mind at ease. "Not the way you're suggesting. But I wouldn't say no to a bit of sparring. I need to do something... real."

Tanny shook her head. "Maybe later. I want to see what's on that data crystal."

"It won't matter," Esper said. "You'll get a chance to look it over and come up with a plan. But Mort's got two options he's going to lay out. Once you've heard them, come find me."

"Come on in," Mort said through the door in reply to Tanny's knock.

The door opened with a familiar creak—the only door on the ship Roddy didn't keep lubricated. "Esper said you had something to talk about. Options?"

"Have a sit," Mort said, patting the bed beside him. He had his shoes and socks off, stretching his toes. He looked all around. "Be it ever so humble, eh?"

Tanny joined him, wondering what had gone on over in Thunderglade. Mort seemed none the worse for wear, at least. "She said you had two competing suggestions."

"Not much for the social niceties, are you?" Mort asked. He lowered his gaze and held up a hand in conciliation. "I'll handle it for you. I had a wonderful time in Thunderglade. The peasants welcomed me back as a lost hero. Keesha missed me dearly, and it was nice to see her again, and I've taken Esper on as my apprentice."

Tanny opened her mouth several times to cut off his smug little rant, but when he finished, her mind went momentarily off course, its autopilot unprepared to react to a wreck in her flight path. "Wait... what?"

"My apprentice," Mort said. "Keesha's putting the paperwork through, so it'll be *her* name on record. But Esper's getting an official Convocation sanction as an apprentice. Who gives a hoot if ARGO thinks she's dead now? Convocation membership will keep them from even checking."

"Is that why she seems different?"

Mort cocked his head. "Does she? I hadn't noticed. Anyway, I'd like to suggest that you take her along to rescue Kubu—just the two of you."

Tanny studied Mort's features. He could keep a straight face as well as just about anyone, except maybe Carl. But she could detect no sign of a joke or any hint of sarcasm. "You're serious."

"It'll be good for her," Mort said. "Seasoning, I think they call it."

"I don't think this is the time—"

"That *makes* it the time. Can't temper steel over a candle flame. Besides, Keesha seemed to think this wouldn't be a big deal. That laaku witch, Inviu, isn't a major threat."

"If I'm bringing a wizard... nothing against Esper, but I'd take you eleven times out of ten," Tanny said. "This isn't a game."

"Well, those are the two options Esper mentioned to you: her or me," Mort said. "But think about this. If you take Esper, you're get Esper, quirks and all. You'll get Kubu back, and odds are no one's going to get killed. If I come, there's a good chance that you, me, and Kubu are the only ones who leave alive."

Tanny gave Mort her best cynical smile. "Nice try, Mort. I know you can find ways around a wholesale slaughter."

Mort crossed his arms. "I'd be ill inclined."

Tanny swallowed and edged away until she was out of arm's reach from the wizard. Easing to her feet, she glided over to the door. "OK, then. I'll give it some thought."

"Go see Esper," Mort said. "I've taught her a trick or three. You won't find her as much of a hindrance as you might imagine."

Tanny slipped on the padded gloves and shoes that were part of her sparring gear, then stepped onto the mat. Esper stood at the far side in pads and workout gear, still proportioned all wrong for a fighter. Thin arms and legs; swollen chest. The opposite would have served her better in combat. Tanny glanced over her shoulder at the catwalk overlooking the cargo hold, to see whether they had an audience. With Carl off who-knows-where, the odds were lower than usual.

"Put a helmet on," Esper said, talking around a mouthguard.

Tanny smirked. "Since when do I need one?" Esper was too slow to land a solid blow unless Tanny let her, and even if she did, between the padded gloves and scrawny arms, she wasn't in any danger.

"Humor me," Esper replied. "I'm planning on trying some things."

"You better not try magicking me," Tanny warned. "Or this'll be the last time we spar."

Esper held up a hand for an oath. "I swear. No magic on you. But Mort wanted me to try using it on myself."

Tanny chuckled. "There's a novel concept."

"Hey," Esper snapped. "You're all hopped up on science drugs. Why not?"

"Should we have Mort standing by, in case you hurt yourself?"

Tanny found her padded training helmet at the bottom of the pile of sparring gear. She hadn't worn it since the last time she's squared off against Mriy, which had been months ago. It stank of stale sweat as she buckled the strap under her chin. A twinge of worry struck her when she saw her own mouthguard in the pile. It was coated in dust, but a quick squirt from her water bottle rinsed it off, and she stuck it in her mouth.

Esper didn't look any different, except for a calmer focus in her eyes. She still stood in a loose stance, hands up at ribcage level. Tanny approached as she often did, at a leisurely saunter. Esper shifted to face Tanny as she stalked around her. Still flat-footed, Tanny saw. She lunged forward with a punch, and Esper shied away, bringing her hands up.

"Sloppy," Tanny said, shaking her head.

Esper responded by feinting a punch, then aiming a kick at Tanny's midsection. Tanny stepped into the kick, caught Esper's foot, and flipped her onto her back. "Whatever you're trying isn't working."

Rolling to the side, Esper scrambled to her feet. "I wasn't trying anything yet." She slurred around the mouthguard, still new at trying to talk while competing. "Still warming up."

This time Esper took up an unfamiliar stance, or at least one Tanny hadn't taught her. It looked like something out of Roddy's martial arts holovids. Standing upright, she had her legs stiff and straight, her hands outstretched in front of her, bobbing like the waves of a harbor.

"You're going to get yourself hurt trying that holovid crap," Tanny scolded.

Esper mumbled something incomprehensible in reply.

"What?"

Spitting the mouthguard onto the cargo bay floor, Esper repeated herself. "Try me."

Tanny obliged, as much out of curiosity as anything. Closing the distance, she threw a probing punch, but Esper batted it aside. A second punch, and Esper tilted her head out of the way. A third never landed because suddenly Tanny's feet weren't under her anymore.

Staring up from the ground, she saw Esper lower the leg that had swept her to the mat. "OK. That worked." She pushed herself to her hands and knees, never taking her eyes from Esper as the apprentice wizard settled back into her casual stance. "Maybe I don't have to take it quite so easy on you. Go ahead and grab that mouthguard."

Esper shook her head.

Tanny wanted to toss hers aside, just to prove her toughness. It was a marine code. In a friendly match, never take an advantage when it's offered. But something told her not to take the risk. Esper hadn't been able to grow Mriy new teeth, and Tanny liked hers well enough to swallow her pride.

The two women squared off again. Tanny came on with a flurry of blows, mixing punches and kicks as Esper blocked and dodged every one of them. Now that Tanny was looking for it, she could tell just how much faster Esper's movements had become. But that was all it was—speed, combined with the adoption of a quirky, holovid style. Tanny baited her into a punch, grabbed a wrist, and flipped Esper to the mat.

Far from accepting the loss of a bout and resetting for a new one, Esper twisted in Tanny's grasp. From the ground, she kicked Tanny's ankles out from under her, breaking the hold and gaining her feet before Tanny could.

Tanny backed off the mat and took out her mouthguard. "What the *fuck* was that? You can't bend like that."

The grin in Esper's eyes begged to differ. She held out her arm and twisted until her hand had spun a complete 360 degrees.

"Don't do that again," Tanny said with a shudder. She's seen limbs torn free from bodies, and bodies with missing limbs, but somehow a living, whole person shouldn't have been able to do that.

Esper held up her hands in apology, then beckoned to Tanny.

The next encounter started much the same, but this time Esper blocked one of Tanny's kicks with a kick of her own, then struck again with the same foot before Tanny could recover. The blow to her midsection drove the air from Tanny's lungs and staggered her, but Esper didn't press the advantage.

"You got bricks in those pads?" Tanny asked between gasps. But it was mere seconds before she had her lungs filled again. Her cocktail of physical-enhancement drugs kept her from being out of any fight while she was still conscious.

This time, Tanny closed quarters with Esper before the apprentice could establish a rhythm on defense. She locked her hands behind Esper's neck and brought a knee up into her midsection. That knee met Esper's crossed wrists instead and stopped dead. Leaving her feet, Tanny brought her other knee up into Esper's face. They fell to the mat together, and Tanny used her momentary advantage to roll Esper facedown and lock an arm around her neck.

That should have been the end of it. Tanny had long since abandoned holding back in the bout. Her combination of arm strength and technique should have forced Esper to either signal her submission or pass out from lack of oxygen. Twin jolts of stabbing pain answered her instead where Esper's elbows hammered into Tanny's ribs. There was a chorus of audible cracks as several broke. As Tanny gritted her teeth against the pain, vise-like fingers pried her arms loose from Esper's neck and shoved her aside.

"I'm sorry. I'm so sorry," Esper said, kneeling over Tanny, blood running from her own broken nose. "That got out of hand." She laid her hands on Tanny's abdomen, just below the fractured ribcage.

It was a bizarre and disquieting sensation as Tanny felt her ribs squirm inside her. Adrenaline alone had kept her from noticing that her ribs hadn't just cracked, but fractured clear through. She braced herself for the ravaging hunger that would soon follow, as her own metabolism sped to supernatural levels to heal her.

But it never came. Esper clasped Tanny's hand and hauled her to her feet. The slip of a girl was like an anchor, not sagging a millimeter under Tanny's weight. "But... how? Shouldn't I be starving now?"

"I've gotten better," Esper said. She wiped a hand under her nose and seemed surprised to see blood. Grabbing her nose, she set it straight, gave it wiggle, and seemed satisfied.

"Mort's some teacher for you to learn so much in a few days," Tanny marveled.

Esper scoffed. "Days? We were gone more than a *year*."

The little room with the letters on the wall was Kubu's least favorite room in Not-Mommy's house. Kubu knew his letters. He knew his numbers, too. Esper had little songs about both of them that made it easy to remember. Not-Mommy didn't like Kubu singing Esper's songs. He sat on a chair and listened while Not-Mommy pointed to pictures in a holovid.

"Apul," Not-Mommy said. She'd taken away his through-the-ear magic for the lesson, and everything was just weird noises. But the picture was an apple. Kubu mimicked the sounds, just trying to get through the lesson.

The image shifted. This time it was a baby version of Kubu's new friend Sumther. It was little and fuzzy, with big ears and dark eyes with no whites around them. "Bair," Not-Mommy said slowly, repeating it several times until Kubu parroted her. It was a silly noise to make for a bear.

"Ket," Not-Mommy said when the holovid turned into a tiny little Mriy. This one walked on all fours and was gray instead of white with patches of orange like Mriy. It was also smiling. Mriy didn't smile like that; hers had more teeth.

It was warm and sunny on the other side of the window. It smelled nice out there. The letters-on-the-wall room smelled like old flowers and lemons—smells Not-Mommy seemed to like better than real smells. Kubu just wanted to go running, maybe eat a bunny or two. There were twenty-six letters though, and there were a lot more left before he could leave.

"Kubu!" Not-Mommy snapped. Kubu's head turned toward the holovid, even though he strained his neck muscles to keep looking out the window. Not-Mommy said a lot of words that Kubu didn't understand, but he understood the idea of the words anyway. There was going to be no playing until he finished his lesson. A low growl rumbled in the back of his throat, and he felt his lip curl to show his teeth. He didn't mean to; it just happened that way.

Kubu knew right away that he'd made a mistake.

Not-Mommy stormed across the room as Kubu whined and tried to make himself smaller. He wagged his tail to show that he hadn't meant it, but they were short, quick wags. Kubu didn't have a big wag in him, or he'd have tried that instead. Not-Mommy grabbed him by the ear and put his through-the-ear magic back in. But she didn't let go of his ear afterward.

"That was very naughty," Not-Mommy told him. This time, Kubu would rather *not* have understood her. "You need some quiet time, then we'll resume the lesson."

Dragged by the ear, Kubu had no choice but to follow Not-Mommy to the quiet room. He looked frantically into the rooms they passed and down each side hallway. Not-Mommy held his ear by the through-the-ear magic, and the tugging hurt as he stumbled awkwardly down the stairs behind her. Kubu whimpered, even though he tried to hold it in.

Not-Mommy pushed him into the quiet room. When Kubu tried to dart through the door before she could close it, his whole body stopped. "You are being punished. If you try to avoid punishment, I will make it worse. You have to learn to respect your elders and to heed me because I am your mother. I have your best interests at heart, but I cannot allow your willfulness to go unchecked. I know you don't like this, but you need to learn that misbehavior has consequences. When you're grown up, the consequences of the real world will not be so kind."

Kubu put his ears back and crouched low, trying to look unthreatening. He cast a baleful look up at Not-Mommy.

But Not-Mommy had a heart a like turtle shell. Nothing could get in when she didn't want it to. She laid a finger firmly atop Kubu's nose; he crossed his eyes to focus on it. "Stay." The thought flashed across his mind to nip at her finger. Not that he wanted to bite it off, just give Not-Mommy a reason not to do it again. But that was just his teeth thinking for him again, and since he'd been living with Not-Mommy his teeth got him into trouble more than they solved anything.

The door closed, and Kubu was alone in the quiet room. The walls were soft, but blank. A weak light in the ceiling kept it from being totally dark; everything was just gloomy and colorless instead. No sounds came in from outside, and no window showed Kubu the outdoors. He was alone.

Kubu was hungry. He was sad and bored and lonely already, and he missed real Mommy. And Esper. And Mort. And even Mriy, Roddy, and Carl a little bit. They were all nicer than Not-Mommy.

He briefly considered pooping in front of the door to get back at Not-Mommy, but realized that he'd probably just get punished again. Worst of all, once she let him out, Not-Mommy was going to bring him right back to his lessons.

After a pair of showers and fresh changes of clothes, Tanny and Esper reconvened in Esper's quarters. Tanny brought two bottles of beer and was mildly surprised when Esper popped the cap off hers with a thumb. The two women sat on the bed —Esper against the wall cushioned by pillows, Tanny at the foot, cross-legged.

"So what was it *like* in there?" Tanny asked. It was weird to contemplate, weirder than most magic she'd heard of. To have spent a year inside Mort's head in the span of a night... no wonder Mort woke up irritable and confused every morning.

Esper sighed and tilted her head back until it rested against the cold metal of the wall. She had aged. Tanny had only known her a few months, and she'd spent three times as long in Mort's dream world. "Ever have one of those dreams where you realize you're dreaming?"

"Kinda, but not really," Tanny said. "Usually wake up as

soon as I notice."

"Same here," Esper said. "But that was how Mort described it. He's been practicing for years. He never said it outright, but I think it has something to do with that book he stole all those years ago."

"But what was it like in there?" Tanny asked. "What does Mort cook up in his dreams?"

"It's sort of like the New Camelot colony, except less wink-and-nod tourist trap and more 'holy shit there are dragons here,'" Esper said, surprising Tanny with her casual vulgarity. "Mort made up everyone there, so the people are a little grumpy and rude. If you think about it, it's like hundreds of Morts all in costume, running around his own head. I had to sort of put that in the back of my mind, or it got creepy."

"Anyone we know?" Tanny asked.

"Everyone we know," Esper said. "Or at least anyone we know that Mort does. They're noblemen and ladies, knights and stablehands. He's got a whole working medieval town and castle in there."

"What am I?" Tanny asked with a smirk. She'd always wondered what Mort really thought of her. The wizard played his cards tight as a miser.

"You're captain of the palace guard," Esper said. "Though it seems mainly honorary. It's Mort's world in there, and he's a hundred times the wizard he is out here. Anyway, you've got this fancy suit of armor and a sword that catches fire on command."

"Smooth," Tanny said. "How about the rest of the crew? Who's Carl?"

"Carl's some nobleman's son," Esper said. "I guess his father is Carl's actual father—Duke Chuck of House Ramsey. Mriy is the game warden. Roddy's the town drunk—please don't tell him I said that. Kubu wasn't around, and Mort said he wanted to keep it that way until we rescued him."

"And you?"

"I was the only real person in there," Esper said. "If I wasn't, he said there was a version of me, too. I was curious to meet my Mort-me, but I'm kinda glad I didn't."

"Do you know what you were?"

"His apprentice already," Esper said. "Not sure how I feel about that. Mort obviously arranged all this ahead of time, but it still feels presumptuous."

Tanny shook her head and took a swig of her beer. "It's *all* fucking presumptuous. Maybe I don't want to be a guard captain, huh? Who's Mort to conscript me?"

"I met his wife," Esper said quietly, changing topics.

"That must have been a trip," Tanny replied. "Mort hasn't seen her in... what? Twenty years? What's she like?"

"She doesn't like me," Esper said. "Mort says he doesn't control the people in his head directly, just makes them up as best he can and turns them loose. And Nancy is jealous; thinks I'm there to replace her. She's sweet and kind and full of laughter when it's just her and Mort, but the second she notices me, she turns into the Ice Death Princess. And of course, she's a wizard, so I had to watch out for her when I was by myself without Mort to protect me."

"Could she have hurt you?" Tanny asked. The rules for living in a dream were unclear. Plenty of holovids had computer-generated worlds with mental selves running around, and they couldn't agree on what happened to someone harmed within the simulation.

"No, but it's hard to think that way when you're inside," Esper said. "Mort promised that the way he brought me in was harmless. He even incinerated me to prove it. I was awake before the flames even hurt. He said there were other ways to inhabit someone else's mind, and not all of them were safe, but that I couldn't be hurt for real. I'm not sure he accounted for body dysmorphism, delusions, or other psychological trauma. I had to use in-dream magic to make myself look right. Mort's mental image of me was close but not perfect, and it was scary looking in a mirror until I fixed it."

"Sounds like Mort's created himself his own little land of accidental horrors," Tanny said. "Glad it's not me who went—no offense."

"Well, learning magic is safe in there," Esper said. "It all works the way Mort thinks it should, which isn't perfect but it's a lot safer than trial and error for real."

Tanny chuckled. "Mort's own personal rules for magic, huh?"

"You laugh, but I think he's more of an expert than he lets on," Esper said.

"Got to you, did he?" Tanny asked. "Mort's always had this sort of low-grade delusion of grandeur, but I think it's rubbing off on you, being in his head. Just don't let him convince you of anything stupid. He may be a wizard, but he's still just an old man."

"Old?" Esper asked. "Don't get me started on old. I aged a year overnight."

"Not really," Tanny said. "I mean, you're acting a little more... I dunno, but different. But you look the same. You didn't get wrinkles or gray hair or anything."

"But I have a year's memories in my head, a year's education and training," Esper said. "It took a month for Mort to finally nail it down that I can't work external magic well because I believe in the real world. But ever since my mother started getting me cosmetic surgery, I've believed that my body is mutable. I can believe in shaping and altering myself. Imagine what I'll learn in a month of nights like that."

Tanny tried. Esper was twenty-four, and a good chunk of that was childhood. Mentally, she'd be in her fifties in a month if she did as she proposed. Or would she still be twenty-four mentally with more than her share of memories? Wasn't there more to mental age than accumulated experience? Dealing with changing life goals and physical and emotional needs was a huge part of aging. Esper waited as she turned the idea over in her head. But try as she might, Tanny couldn't predict what would happen. "Crazy," she said at last.

"Crazy?" Esper asked. "I did some quick math. Assuming Mort started learning how to do this twenty years ago, starting from essentially zero time dilation and extending his nights arithmetically longer ever since, until he can manage a year a night now..."

"Sure," Tanny said. It was easy at times to forget that Esper had been a math teacher at that One Church school on Bentus VIII. Tanny hadn't quite followed the logic, but she assumed Esper was right about it, whatever it was.

"Well, that would mean that *mentally*, Mort is something like 3,650 years old."

Tanny spent the evening hours in her quarters poring over her datapad, scanning news feeds and decrypted rebroadcasts of law-enforcement channels. Passive stuff. Anything that required a query to the omni was liable to be monitored. It didn't take any personnel resources by the Phabian Intelligence Service to keep tabs on her outgoing omni use, just tech. And they had plenty of tech to throw around.

After an initial burst-dam flood of speculation surrounding the investigation of Carl's crash, things had gone quiet—eerily quiet. It wasn't that the crackpots and demagogues weren't still spouting their usual vitriol, but the respectable sources had clammed up. The official sources weren't putting out any more updates on the investigation. For an outfit that boasted of openness and transparency, it was ominous. When an organization with a motto of "Trust, Integrity, Justice" wasn't willing to comment on the case, it was a bad sign.

"They've got to have started putting it together," Tanny muttered. But that didn't explain everything. It was just a thread to tug on. "But if they did, why aren't we in custody? Why was Chuckles the Interrogation Monkey going through the checklist instead of calling in backup? It's not like they don't have the manpower."

She shut off the datapad and dropped it on the bed.

Why was it that stress made her thirsty? Was it even thirst? Tanny counted the empty bottles and cans on the floor. Four beers since her sparring session with Esper, not including the one she drank in Esper's quarters and discarded in the waste processor. Was she turning into Roddy?

"No more beer tonight," she promised herself.

But the thirst was still there, so she ventured out to the common room in search of what the fridge might have to offer. She could hear the muffled sound of shouts and blaster fire and knew that someone was out there already. Turned out that it was Roddy, watching a fists-and-blasters action holo.

"Hey-o!" he called out when Tanny stepped from her quarters. He waved her over with what appeared to be a bacon-and-pickle sandwich. With one foot he paused the holovid by remote. "I can back it up if you want. *Combat Lord Jhunzin Versus the Zheen*. I'm only five minutes in." He separated a can from the six-pack next to him on the couch and lobbed it her way.

It was so easy. A pop-top and one smooth motion of the

hand and beer would pour into her. It would take the edge off the worries that the Cannabinol in her drug regimen couldn't. Brute force. If tailored psychiatric drugs weren't getting the job done with precision strikes, she could bomb her troubles from orbit.

She tossed the can back. "Sorry. Gotta keep it together. If Carl gets back here, Squall or no Squall, we're off this rock."

"What about Mriy?"

"I'm hoping that datapad caddy from Phabian spooks her into heading back here before then," Tanny said. "If not... maybe we make a stop along the way. We've taken bigger detours during getaways."

Tanny found a grapefruit-flavored EnerJuice in the fridge —undoubtedly Esper's doing—and joined Roddy on the couch. She didn't make him restart the holo, but she let herself slip into the bland, waking comatose of mindless entertainment. The laaku warlord in the holo-field was cutting a swath through blaster-toting Zheen soldiers with his bare hands. The choreography was top-notch. Aside from being preternaturally strong and fast, Combat Lord Jhunzin was making sound tactical decisions, prioritizing targets, and making proper use of cover and environmental factors. He wasn't flipping around like the monks in *Four Fists, Zero Fear*, or counting on his enemies having lousy aim the way Kickmaster Thulau seemed to. Jhunzin was a DNA-upgraded laaku veteran of a dozen wars, sleeping in the cryostasis chamber in between so he was always ready when Phabian needed a hero.

The holo echoed true for Tanny. There was a lot of marine in Jhunzin. He was science-modified, had given up home and family to defend his way of life, and no one seemed to appreciate the gravity of his sacrifice. Tanny might have been a notch off her peak since her days in the service, but it wasn't a big notch. She'd had top-notch training in hand-to-hand combat, endured physical alterations at the hands of ARGO's bio-improvement division, and became dependent on a regimen of expensive chemicals that altered not just her physiology, but her brain chemistry.

The holovid froze. "Hey, Countess," Roddy called out as Esper shuffled past in slippers and pajamas. "Where you headed?" Roddy's smirk and glance at the overnight bag that Esper clutched to her chest said he already had his answer, but wanted to hear her say it.

"Off to my next lesson," Esper replied, turning her head to stifle a yawn against her arm. She resumed her sleepy trek in the direction of Mort's quarters. There was brief eye contact between her and Tanny. In that one look, Tanny knew that Esper was leaving it to her to tell Roddy whatever she liked.

The door to Mort's quarters opened, then shut.

"So that's the story they're going with?" Roddy asked. "Weak."

There was a sensitive soul somewhere inside that laaku mechanic. Tanny had heard him play guitar—songs that he'd written—and make himself cry. There was some quantity of alcohol necessary to bring that out in him. It wasn't zero, and it didn't sound like it was the amount in him currently.

"Carl owes me fifty terras, you know," Roddy said, leaning close. "He bet me Mort wasn't sleeping with her. Looks like he was wrong about her, huh?" Roddy elbowed Tanny conspiratorially. "You want a sure bet, long term? Every time you got the chance to bet whether two humans are going at it, bet yes. You'll take it on the chin once in a while, but keep making that bet and it'll pay you back with interest. You freaks breed like roaches."

Tanny waggled her can of EnerJuice to see how much was left. After tilting it back and sucking the last drops from the bottom, she sighed and took one of Roddy's beers. "I guess technically you're right. But it's not what you think. Hell, I think we've been wrong about *both* of them."

There were times when Carl wished that he had a nice, normal job. He could have run a bar and spent the day trading gossip and shooting pool. If he'd gone into comedy like his father, he could still travel, and scrape by as he saw the seedy backstage scene from one end of the galaxy to the other. Hell, he could even have decided to run a legitimate cargo service—he already had a ship for it. None of those careers would have resulted so frequently in being arrested, detained, and generally on the blaster-point end of the law enforcement system.

Waking up strapped to his hospital bed had given Carl time to ponder those alternate career options. Right about then he was considering whether he'd even get a chance to decide between prison mess hall and laundry detail. Prisons weren't renowned for their congenial employment programs.

The room was dim, with the overhead lights off and just a halo of light peeking around the curtains. If the facility was as modern as the doctor had boasted it was under the surface, they must have been monitoring his vitals. They must have realized he was awake and aware. A few experimental tugs told Carl that he was going nowhere. The cuffs on his wrists and ankles were thickly-padded leather, just loose enough to allow for circulation and tight enough that he could barely flex his fingers or wiggle his toes.

"Water," he croaked to no one in particular. He wasn't thirsty, per se, but he played it up for sympathy in case anyone *was* watching over him. There was an IV tube in his arm. Since he'd woken up, it was probably straight saline, no sedatives. Other tubes had made sure he didn't soil himself while comatose.

A minute or so later, the door opened and the lights flicked on. Carl blinked at the sudden brightness. A young nurse stepped in with a datapad in hand, its wood trim trying but failing to make it resemble an old-fashioned clipboard. "Good morning, Mr. Doe," she said. "How are you feeling?"

"Thirsty," Carl replied. "And a little claustrophobic. Think you could let me up?" He smiled his best inoffensive smile at the nurse. She could have been a doctor in disguise, like Dr. Singh. But she looked legitimately young and not cosmo young like Esper; probably too young to have finished medical school, burnt out on civilized life, and moved out to the retroverse already.

"I'll get you some water," the nurse replied. "But I'm afraid I can't release those restraints, Mr. Doe. Dr. Singh's orders."

"Why do you keep calling me Mr. Doe?" Carl asked. Had he been mislabeled? Was some poor bastard being arrested as Carl Ramsey in another room? It might be worth playing along if this Doe guy wasn't scheduled for a vasectomy or a sex change, or anything else unpleasant.

"Would you prefer John?" she asked. "I try not to get too familiar with patients. It's not very Americana, you know?"

Carl let his head slump back against the pillow. John Doe. Of course. Dr. Singh didn't have a name to admit him under, not one she was willing to place on file anyway. When in doubt, she went the cliché road and labeled him a John Doe. He wondered if the nurse even knew the lingo, or if she thought that was really his name. She was probably interning here as if it were low-development sentient world in need of interplanetary aid. A social-conscience do-gooder with no sense of the vibe of the colony.

"John's fine," he said.

She brought him water, and a while later a breakfast of oatmeal topped with cinnamon. It didn't seem all that nutritious for hospital food, but she denied it when he accused her of serving him reconstituted laaku fare. Those machines of theirs could turn just about anything organic into raw nutrients, then put it back together looking and tasting like almost anything else. It was bad enough thinking about some small percentage of it was laaku remains, recycled "for the good of the people," but the bulk of it was insectile in origin.

It was hours later before anyone else arrived. In the meantime, Carl was subject to the humiliations of the bedpan and continued intrusion of a catheter. Not to mention that there was still an IV dripping into his arm that may or may not have been entirely saline. But eventually Dr. Singh arrived. With her was a plainclothes police officer. Carl knew even before the cop ID'ed himself. He'd seen enough period flatvids to know the cheap suit-and-tie combo, not to mention the slight bulge of a holster by the guy's armpit.

The door closed behind them. "Mr. Ramsey, this is Detective Sullivan from the Anaheim PD," Dr. Singh said.

Carl closed his eyes. "So, you're working for them."

"Mr. Ramsey," Detective Sullivan said. He had the voice of a twenty-year smoker. "We've been looking into this story of yours. I was hoping you might be able to... clear a few things up. Things I'm not clear on."

"Not a lot to be clear on here," Carl said. "I'm here. Some clone of me is dead. What? You think *I* killed him?"

"I think you know more than you're letting on," Detective Sullivan said. "For starters, what are you doing here on Peractorum in the first place?"

"I spent some time here as a kid," Carl said. He didn't even need to think up a lie for that one. "Figured it was a low-key locale to let the shit-storm blow over. I got a sister around here

I haven't seen in a while. Figured I'd say hi to her before I moved along, but you fine folks snagged me before I even made a phone call."

Phone call... Carl was starting to form the rudimentary core of a plan.

"And it's a coincidence that your ship, the *Mobius*, is on-world not two-hundred miles from here?" Detective Sullivan asked.

Carl perked up. No reason for *them* to know it wasn't news to him. "The *Mobius* is here? Great! Just let me get some clothes on, and I'll get out of your hair." He shook one restrained hand to draw attention to his continued confinement.

"Not so fast," Detective Sullivan said. "There's still plenty here that doesn't add up."

Carl looked past Detective Sullivan to Dr. Singh. "Did you get the low-down on the Phabian investigation? That should clear me."

Dr. Singh pursed her lips. "I couldn't get past the front door making comms to my friends there. But what I *was* able to find out is that it's Harmony Bay who's running interference."

"There you go!" Carl said. "Just like I said. That proves I'm telling you the truth." Vehement denial and proclamations of innocence worked sometimes, but they were better on soft hearts like Dr. Singh. Detective Sullivan was hard-boiled and fresh from a pulp novel; he'd be ornery just because it's in the job description. Still, one ally might be all he needed in the end. Even that nurse might have been enough. And thank God for Harmony Bay being their usual, dickish bully selves about the whole thing. They couldn't help themselves getting involved. It was like a despotic corporate reflex, like swatting at mosquitoes.

"That proves you knew one player in this," Detective

Sullivan said. He leaned close, looming over Carl. Mriy would have bitten him at this range. Tanny would have head-butted him and broken his nose. Carl had to just push his head back deeper into the pillows as Detective Sullivan edged closer. "But I'll make you a deal. A chance to prove you're telling me the truth."

"Oh?" Carl asked. He tried to sound worried. But if he couldn't beat a twentieth-century polygraph test, he had no business in this line of work.

"Detective Sullivan is a wizard," Dr. Singh said.

"So the, 'I can look into your head and see you thinking' thing," Carl replied. "Neat trick, but isn't that *way* illegal? I have rights."

"Rights?" Detective Sullivan asked, standing upright and giving Carl room to breathe. "Sure you got rights. I can march you down to the precinct in handcuffs, throw you in a cell, and get you indicted for vehicular theft. Then I can make a few comms, and Phabian Investigative Service is probably going to pull rank on me and demand we extradite you. And me, being a small-town cop who isn't paid to deal with that sort of shitstorm, I say 'sure,' and they pick you up. Then you can deal with them instead of me."

"Fine," Carl said. "I've got nothing to hide."

"Smart, kid," Detective Sullivan said. "Real smart. Now just breathe deep and relax, and look into my eyes."

Mort had hammered it into Carl's head from a young age: never look a wizard in the eyes. It was good, general purpose advice, like looking both ways before crossing the street or making sure your blaster was charged before a fight. But shit happens, rules are made to be broken, and Carl didn't think Detective Sullivan was wizard enough to fry an egg.

Carl felt the intrusion as Detective Sullivan's eyes met his own. He told himself that he'd escaped from a ship called the

Bradbury, owned by Harmony Bay. There was a lab there, with tanks and vats and bubbling liquids pumped through clear hoses. Men and women in monochrome jumpsuits monitored equipment, their faces obscured by sterile masks. In his imagination, Carl slipped around behind the tanks, staying out of sight. Bare feet slapped quietly against the cold floor. In one of the tanks, just millimeters away through the glass wall, a human form floated, suspended in green fluid.

The puppet show in Carl's head continued. He ran through corridors without knowing where he was going. A scientist came by, and Carl hid around a corner, ambushed him, and took his uniform. Using a stolen keycard, he gained access to a cargo bay and hid himself inside a container designated for delivery. He hastily added a quick bartered trip aboard a smuggler's ship, a stowaway passage on another, and a cheap flight to Peractorum to catch Detective Sullivan up to where things stood now.

All this while, as Carl convinced himself that this all really happened, he ushered the actual memories from that time period into a broom closet and told them to shut up for a little while. With facts out of the way, Carl felt a lot more heroic and paranoid about his harrowing escape.

Detective Sullivan broke the contact with a gasp and stumbled back a step from Carl.

"What'd you find out?" Dr. Singh asked.

Detective Sullivan stood there, shaking his head in disbelief. "I don't know what this all means. But this guy's telling the truth about Harmony Bay being out to get him."

"So, I'm free to go?" Carl asked.

Detective Sullivan's confidence returned with a smirk. "And what about that theft charge? Maybe you think I was gonna let you off on account of a hard-luck story?"

"At least let me get dressed before you take my mug shot,"

Carl said. This time period had so many holes in its legal system, you could strain pasta with it. The theft rap was a loser in court, and it would never get that far. Any first-year law student could get him off. Fortunately for Carl, he had a boyfriend-in-law who fit that bill. "And I get one phone call, don't I?"

Roddy was cleaning up in the cargo bay when Mriy returned. Most of the star-drive was reassembled in roughly the configuration he'd found it, and the few leftover components he would store in a locker until he decided where to weld, bolt, or jam them into the mechanism. It was all for show anyway, much the way he suspected Mriy's uniform was.

"What's with the getup?" Roddy asked by way of greeting. "There a prison detail I didn't know about? I thought it was black and white stripes around this place." Mriy wore an all-orange costume that fit loose around the body, but was tied close against her lower legs and belted in black cloth. He knew exactly what it was from having watched humanity's take on martial arts holos, but he couldn't resist the jab.

"I was imprisoned briefly for devouring a know-it-all mechanic," Mriy replied with a toothy snarl. "Or was that just a vision of the future I had during meditation? Time will reveal," she added with a shrug.

Roddy wiped his hands on a rag and followed her up to the common room. "How was Kung-Fu Land? You beat up anyone interesting?"

"Master Lao was a more able combatant than Tanny,"

Mriy replied. "I was not allowed to spar with the other pupils. He said I lacked control, so he paired me with himself."

Roddy detoured to the fridge as Mriy opened the door to her quarters to throw her duffel inside. "'Lacked control' being a euphemism for an azrin getting pissed off and clawing some poor shit's throat out when she starts losing?"

"Possibly," Mriy admitted with a grin. "But that bare-headed little man was impossible to strike, and he had knuckles like steel."

"They're all wizards, you know," Roddy said. "According to Mort, all that chi doesn't move on its own."

"Mort thinks that breathing is magic," Mriy replied. She fished a beer of her own from the fridge and claimed a swath of couch.

"That's true," Mort said as the door to his quarters opened. "You might want to summon the girls on the talk-box," he mentioned to Roddy.

With a shrug, Roddy activated the comm panel for ship-wide broadcast. "Hail, hail, the gang's all here. Well, all but Carl." He hopped onto one of the kitchen chairs and tipped it back onto two legs. Balancing it in place was a simple reflex—he didn't need to lean it against the wall or put his feet up on the table the way Carl did.

Moments later, Esper emerged from her quarters and Tanny joined them from the cockpit. "Welcome back," Tanny said when she saw Mriy. "Have fun punching little bald guys?"

Mriy flattened her ears back. "They were worthy warriors. Don't make light of them."

"Warriors use guns these days," Tanny said. "Hand-to-hand is a backup option. Those guys are sportsmen, not fighters."

"Try one of them yourself," Mriy countered. "See how

you fare."

"Naw," Roddy said. "She got her ribs busted by Esper yesterday. I don't think she's up to snuff for kung-fu masters."

"How'd you know about that?" Tanny demanded.

Roddy hated being on the business end of her temper. He raised his hands in surrender. "Hey, I just—"

"Did *you* tell him?" Tanny snapped at Esper.

Esper retreated a step and shook her head.

"He records all the girl-fights in the cargo bay," Mort said. "Him and Carl. Despicable, the both of them."

Roddy's eyes went wide. "You watch them, too!" It was one thing sneaking a holo feed when it was all fun and entertainment. It was another dumping a confession at the foot of the angriest woman on board.

"You *what*?"

Mriy's purr-like snickering broke the tension. "Carl still seeks pleasure in your form."

"Esper," Tanny said. "Dig through the computer and see what they've been recording. If there isn't anything topless, I *might* not decide to break any arms over this."

"Uh, OK," Esper said. "But maybe we should think about Kubu. Mriy's back. Maybe we let Carl hide out while we go rescue him. Then we can come back and pick up Carl before he gets into too much trouble."

"You got a plan yet?" Roddy asked. Tanny'd been beating herself up over rescuing Kubu, but every chance she got, she shot outside the firing range about something completely unrelated. That dog of hers was going to be the death of someone, whether it was his own jaws or Tanny's mothering instincts making her stupid and careless.

"We get close, take assumed IDs, swap to local transport, get planetside, take care of business, and the *Mobius* swoops in for a pickup," Tanny said. "I've got the details sorted out, but that's the barstool version. Two-man extraction team, just me and Mort."

"Whatever you say," Mort said. But Roddy heard the careful-what-you-wish-for lilt that made him question whether Mort really meant a word of it. "As soon as we get Carl back."

Tanny scowled at the wizard. "We've already sat on this rock long enough with our tits flapping in the wind. We don't *need* Carl for this plan. He can vacation in the Stone Age with his toy raceship for a few days. If I had a way to contact him, I would. But I'm not waiting for that inconsiderate ass to waltz back here before we go find Kubu."

"All well and good," Mort said. "But I'll wait here for Carl. Maybe even go looking for him."

"My tits aren't flapping," Roddy muttered into his beer before taking a sip, not making eye contact with anyone.

"Maybe you've missed the comm, Mort, but we can't drop astral without you on board," Tanny said. "This isn't a cryostasis barge. We don't have months to spend limping there in realspace."

"Let Esper do it," Mort said.

"Since when does *she* know how to impersonate a stardrive?" Tanny asked, spreading her arms.

"*She* is standing not ten feet from you," Mort replied. "Try asking her instead of me. She's not furniture, or some kitchen gewgaw. She's a fledgling wizard."

"I learned last night," Esper replied. "I'm... not very good at it yet."

"Wonderful," Tanny muttered.

Mort wagged a finger. "Humility is the devil's quagmire. Confidence—"

"Is the fuel of success," Esper finished with an air of resignation. "I know, but truth has to factor in somewhere."

"Not if Carl's any benchmark," Roddy mumbled.

"Besides," Mort said. "You'll need a wizard along to counter Inviu. Esper can manage that just fine."

"I'm guessing this Inviu has a little more practice under her belt," Tanny said. "Maybe some real-world experience?"

"Esper may be raw, but she's human, with a proper human imagination," Mort said. "She can pin Inviu's magic to reality just fine. Laaku struggle letting go of science; it gets pounded into them too deep as kids."

"Here, here!" Roddy toasted, raising his can of Earth's Preferred. "To science! And the stuff it brews!"

"Sorry," Tanny said. "I'm not having your first try taking a ship into astral space be the *Mobius* without Mort aboard."

Esper clasped her hands together with a quick glance at the ceiling. "Thank you."

"So no dice, Mort," Tanny said. "We need you. Without Carl here, I'm acting captain. Do I have to make this an order?"

Mort snorted. "If you need me, I'll be roaming New Cali, looking for Carl." He opened the door to his quarters.

"Mort, don't you walk away from me," Tanny shouted. She followed him and pounded on the door after it closed behind him. "Mort, this is mutiny! Mort? *Moooort*!"

The door opened moments later. Mort wore a button-down shirt and slacks. His tie was black silk, and his cuff links bore little Convocation sigils. He shrugged into a tweed jacket as he pushed past Tanny.

"Mort, we need your help on this," Tanny said, her face flushed from her shouting.

Mort patted her on the cheek. "No, you don't. You've got everything you need right here. Old Mort won't be around forever, and you can't get dependent on me. And to think, I promised you if you had me along I'd kill everyone in that little compound of hers, and you still picked me over Esper. I'm not sure which troubles me more, you thinking I was that sort of monster, or that you still wanted my help."

They watched in silence as Mort left the common room and waited until the sound of his footsteps was too faint to hear through the closed door. Even without magic, Mort had a way of exerting the force of his personality over the ship.

Tanny's wildfire had burnt itself out. She turned to Esper. "You still up for this?"

Esper swallowed and gave a quick nod. "I'll do my best."

"Good," Tanny said. "Pack your gear. We're taking public transit the whole way."

Mort looked over his shoulder, unable to shake the feeling that someone was following him. It was dusk, and the lights from restaurants and storefronts lit the sidewalks that he strolled. Whether this was supposed to be a replica New York, Chicago, Los Angeles, or just some generic city with a Prime sensibility to it, Mort couldn't say. There were pedestrians on all sides, cars whizzing up and down the streets—if those had been hovering a yard over the road, it would have felt like Boston Prime. He could see how people could fall in love with a place like this.

He rounded a corner and ducked into the entryway of a barber shop, looming over an elderly man sitting on the stoop and reading a newspaper. "If you're lookin' for a trim, better get yourself inside," the man said. "Saul's closin' up soon; it's bowling night."

Mort spared the man a glance before he returned his attention to the way he came. He didn't see anyone suspicious coming. "No. Hair's fine. That today's paper?"

"Evening edition of the Tribune," the man replied, eyeing him up and down. "You wander off the tour? I don't remember seeing you around here."

"Something like that," Mort replied. "I'm looking for a friend who got lost. Thinks he's some sort of James Dean. Anything in there about a guy fresh from deep space wandering the colony?"

"Not that I saw," the man replied. "Welcome to have a look for yourself, if you want to sit a spell. I'm just readin' up on last night's scores. Cubbies done lost another one in extras."

"Thanks," Mort said, taking the front section the man offered. The headline was about a local election coming up, and below the fold was a story about progress on a housing development. "By the by, what gave me away?"

"What, that you weren't from these parts?" the man asked. "Shoot, you got the look almost perfect, but you don't act like you live here. Besides, one little detail done gave you away."

"What's that?"

"Them fancy-pants cuff links," the man said. "Shoot, I bet you most folks these parts never seen a Convocation man before. But I wasn't born back in time. New Orleans Prime, born and bred." The pronunciation without the 'r' and condensed to two syllables led Mort to believe the man had at least been there.

As Mort looked down at the front page of the Tribune and its headline about a local mayoral election, something caught the corner of his eye. There was a nun standing on the street corner, huddled against the pole of a traffic light. Her head was down, casting her face in the shadows of her habit.

But the shape was off. There was a slouch and hunched shoulders that fit poorly with the prim and self-conscious imagine of the sisters of the cloth. A fleeting guess that Esper had followed him fizzled the instant he put it to the test of logic. She wouldn't hunch or huddle, and the lack of curves was a giveaway. If Esper had used magic to alter her appearance, he'd have known immediately; that girl's magic was as subtle as the police siren wailing two blocks away.

"Sorry, I've got to run," Mort said, handing the newspaper back.

"Go on, keep it," the man replied. "I already read that section."

Mort muttered a quick thanks and stalked over to confront the suspicious nun. There was decorum to consider when lambasting a holy woman in public, but Mort wasn't planning to stick around New Cali long enough to suffer the long-term consequences of maligning an upstanding member of the community if it turned out he was wrong.

"The bloody hell you doing following me?" Mort demanded in a harsh whisper once he was a mere pace away.

"Follow me into the alley," Mriy replied. Her growling voice was unmistakable.

Mort did as she asked and joined her in a narrow alleyway between a pizzeria and a record store. It was just a paved corridor containing a dumpster and several steel trash cans. "You pea-brained fool," he scolded. "Don't you know they don't like anyone but humans and the occasional laaku around here? You're liable to run into some golly-gosh-jeepers cop who's never been off-world and scare the bullets out of his gun."

Mriy shook her head, dismissing Mort's objections. "You must have followed the same trail I did. Carl was seen at a drinking and gaming place named after a shark and was arrested after trying to steal a vehicle of some sort."

"Trail?" Mort asked. "This is the third city I've been to. I just took a map and looked from the starship parking lot to see where Carl might have headed."

"When I caught your scent, I assumed—"

"Where the hell did you get that penguin suit, anyway?" Mort asked. "No, forget I asked that. I don't like answering that sort of question, so I won't hypocrify myself."

"Carl is being held in a jail not far from here," Mriy said. "Had I not caught scent of you, I would have made the rescue on my own. With your help, it should go more easily."

"Goes without saying..." Mort muttered.

"He is charged in the theft of a vehicle," Mriy said. "He was injured, but has recovered. We should find him fit to retrieve."

"Well then, what are we waiting for?" Mort asked. "Aside from maybe a less conspicuous disguise for you."

Mriy backed away a step. "Not like last time."

"Last time was just pretty colors," Mort said. "Those pirates *believed* in azrin. We can't have the local retroverts seeing an off-world sentient. It would be nice if we didn't narrow the lists of jailbreak suspects *quite* so much for retro-police. This might seem like a theme park, but we kick a hornet's nest hard enough, we'll get ARGO up our asses."

"That little laaku with the datapad was a pest," Mriy said. "I don't want to get jailed among Roddy's kind."

"Then stick close, don't draw attention to us," Mort said, rubbing his chin. He considered Mriy's size, build, and general disposition. "And if you think you can act like Tanny's cousin Jimmy..."

"The son of her Uncle Earl?" Mriy asked.

"That's the one. You'll look like him, so just act like an angry business suit stuffed full of meat and keep your mouth shut."

"Can't you think of a female disguise?" Mriy grumbled.

Mort chuckled. "You look around this place at all? You don't fit what they think of as a woman. I can magic you up a frilly dress, high heels, and red lipstick, but I don't see you playing the part. Now hold still..."

Kubu watched the birds fly past overhead, one chasing the other. Since they were the same size with feathers the same shade of blue, Kubu assumed they were playing, not hunting one another. People weren't supposed to eat their own kind, Kubu had been told by both Mommy and Not-Mommy, and he supposed that it applied to animals as well. Kubu envied them, way up in the sky, going wherever they wanted.

"Whatcha looking at, big guy?" Chimjo asked. Not-Mommy's assistant always followed Kubu around outside. It wasn't as if he were going to get lost. Chimjo might have been a friend if he either didn't talk at all, or could understand Kubu. One-way talking wasn't very friendly.

Kubu scowled up at the birdies, a low growl in his throat. What were their names again? "Two... bird," he said, using Not-Mommy's lesson words.

"Those are tarquils," Chimjo said. Kubu knew it was a lie, since they were very clearly birds. "Mrs. Inviu had them brought in and resettled from Ganges IV. They were dying out, but nothing she's got here will hunt them."

"Kubu... bird?" Kubu asked. There were so many missing words in Not-Mommy's language. Some he couldn't remember, some he didn't know at all. How could Kubu explain to Chimjo that he wanted to fly away, find the flying house, and go live with Mommy again?

"Aw, you don't want to eat those," Chimjo said. The

thought *had* occurred to Kubu. "There aren't enough on the whole planet to make a meal for you. Plus, you're not too selective about your hunting, and those little guys are mostly feathers."

"Kubu... am... bird?"

Chimjo laughed. "Not likely. You're a canid. That's a family with dogs and wolves and that sort of animal. Birds've got hollow bones and feathers and wings. You've got two-hundred kilos of muscle and four legs. You're not getting airborne without a ship."

"Kubu... want... am... bird."

"No, you don't," Chimjo said. "Flying without a ship might look like fun, but what kinda price you willing to pay for it? Those tarquils up there are dumb little buggers. Brains the size of a Chew-Pop. No hands, no teeth, no claws. All they eat is insects and seeds. You think anything that small's gonna eat a rabbit? Or a deer? All they can do is fly away and hide if anything tries to eat them, and they're lousy at it. But Mrs. Inviu doesn't like things dying out, so she brought a bunch of the daft critters here to keep 'em safe. You? You're sentient. You're going to grow up huge. Then you can make a living doing what you want—probably something in the area of personal security for someone with loads of terras. Don't envy the damn birds over one stupid trick."

Kubu cast his eyes down. "Sorry." He learned that word early on. It was probably the most useful word Not-Mommy had taught him.

"Come on," Chimjo said. "We ought to get back inside. You've got lessons in ten minutes."

Kubu sighed and fell into step behind Chimjo. He didn't feel like racing back to the house today. As he loped along, he looked up to the sky. Even if flying was a stupid trick, those birdies looked happy up there.

Mort and the disguised Mriy loitered on a park bench across from the police station. It was a red-brick building, compact and functional, with a row of squad cars parked out front. Strip away the signage and remove the marked vehicles, and it could have been a public library. The setting sun cast the upper floor and roof in a pinkish light.

"I don't suppose it's the sort of place where they close down for the night," Mort said quietly, during a break in the pedestrian traffic.

"Not from anything I've watched," Mriy replied. "They seem to have copied everything from holovids, but this isn't my field of expertise."

"Well, if either of us has watched enough bloody holos, we ought to be able to plan a simple jailbreak," Mort said. It wasn't as if they lacked for resources. A few police officers with primitive science guns weren't much of a threat. As much as Mriy looked like Tanny's gangster goon cousin Jimmy at the moment, she was still an azrin. And while Mort wasn't terribly interested in drawing attention to the fact that a wizard was invading from New Camelot, he wasn't about to let that stop him from busting Carl out of jail.

"Wouldn't these colonists be familiar with those tricks?" Mriy asked.

"Hell. Probably," Mort said. "Maybe it's better if we try something original."

"I'm all ears," Mriy replied, drawing a grin from Mort. It wasn't often she pulled out a human idiom, but this one contained a nugget of an idea.

"How good *are* those ears of yours?" Mort asked. "Think you can hear through a brick wall?"

"I'm not familiar with ancient human building materials,"

Mriy said. "But this bench is uncomfortable, and I tire of waiting. No one around here serves decent food, and I haven't eaten since morning. I'd be willing to eat a few of these police guards right now."

"Cap those fangs, Miss Carnivore," Mort said. "These backwater retroverts are just playing out their little game world. Those cops are just soldiers doing a job. Not to mention that Carl's almost surely guilty of whatever they caught him at."

"It's Carl," Mriy agreed with a nod. "I had assumed so as well."

"Well, just mind that we're not exactly the forces of law and justice in this little holovid," Mort said. "Sympathy for killing law enforcement usually ends at corruption. These kindly bumpkins might decide to call in for off-world backup if we kick them hard enough."

Mriy growled a sigh. "Agreed."

As dusk settled in, the wizard and disguised azrin strolled around the side of the building. Mort had a pleasant conversation with the streetlamps and moonlight, persuading them to look elsewhere to cast their revealing glows. Meanwhile, Mriy probed the outside walls of the police station, pressing a sensitive feline ear against the brick.

Mort kept silent and waited. He knew that if she heard anything worth mentioning, she'd say so. Unlike certain other members of the *Mobius* crew, he knew how to hold his tongue. Pestering her with questions would only slow things down and possibly alert any officers within earshot.

"I think I've located him," Mriy whispered, ear still resting against the outside wall. "I can't hear what he's saying, but I recognize the cadence of the voice. He's not alone. There are two other... make that three others with him. Male. Human. I can't make out much else."

"How sure are you that it's Carl?"

Mriy shrugged. "You want to wait out here all night?"

"Good point," Mort replied. "They might move him, then we'd be starting over if we come back to this spot later. Stand back."

Mort wondered at the mortar. Such a curious thing, how a bunch of gloppy gray mud could hold bricks together to make a solid wall. It strained credulity. And even the bricks themselves were just baked clay. If Mort left a bunch of clay out in the sun, it wouldn't turn into anything sturdy enough to serve as a wall. Someone really ought to check into whether this wall was really a wall at all. What if it was just a stack of brittle clay blocks, held loosely in place with mud?

Holding a hand to the wall, Mort stepped back, and a section the size of a large doorway came free, stuck to his hand as if by suction cup. With a simple trick of logic, Mort insisted that *he* wasn't the one holding up that unreasonable weight of bricks; they were all holding each other up, in a twisted loop of broken causality that continued to work because of the plain evidence that they already were.

Mort swung the section of wall aside as the occupants of the room beyond let out vulgar shouts of surprise and disbelief. Carl was inside, sitting at a shabby table wearing handcuffs. Lloyd was seated beside him, and across from them were two fellows in uniformly cheap suits. With a subtle reminder to the universe that the bricks were just held together with mud, the section of wall Mort had removed fell apart into individual bricks, which shattered to reddish crumbs as they hit the ground.

"What the hell's going on here?" one officer shouted, he knocked his chair over leaping to his feet.

His companion was quicker and already had his gun drawn from its holster. He fired it at Mriy as the azrin in gangster's clothing rushed him. Two shots. One shot whizzed past Mort; the other did not. A third shot flew harmlessly into the far wall as Mriy drove the detective to the ground.

Carl knocked over the table and curled into a ball behind the cover it provided. Lloyd rolled out of his chair and joined him in a low crouch.

The second detective was slower to get his gun out, but Mort was tired of primitive weapons. He'd assumed—wrongly, it seemed—that the amount of magic he'd used would have rendered their weapons inoperable. Apparently he hadn't damaged local physics badly enough to prevent whatever science made bullets work. As the second detective turned his firearm on Mriy in an effort to help his companion, the steel turned to dripping molten ore in his hand.

"Ow! Shit," the detective exclaimed as he dropped the melted weapon.

"Glad to see you found me," Carl said from the floor. There were a lot of things to be said about Carl, but he was a pro. There was no use of names, no "Mort, I'm so glad to see you. Where's the *Mobius*?" He'd let himself be rescued before he worried about what was going on.

"You must be Mort," Lloyd said from the floor. "I've heard so much about you. Where's the *Mobius*? Looks like we're down this whole jailbreak path now, huh?"

"For what it's worth," Carl said. "I had faith that you'd have gotten me off. It was a bullshit charge, and these chuckleheads knew it."

There was already a commotion in the station at large. Probably a response to shots being fired in an interrogation room. It seemed silly in a way, since Mort's magic was by far the larger threat. It was like arresting jaywalkers during a riot. Still, Mort supposed that what they didn't know was probably going to hurt them, and he'd already burned the hand of one poor slob just earning a paycheck.

"If you two boys would like to use that door, now's the time," Mort said.

The detective with the burned hand looked down at the floor, where Mriy was rising from the limp form of his partner. It was an incongruous sight, seeing a thick-necked, muscle-bound human with his fingers and mouth bloody. Mort had grown accustomed to Mriy to the point where he'd stopped cringing at her close-combat methods. Seeing a human who'd bitten and clawed another was far more disturbing. "There's just one," Mriy said. "Fucker shot me."

Mort gave the remaining detective a rueful smile. "Looks like we've got a countdown," Mort said. "Care to be on it?"

"We shouldn't stay here," Lloyd said. "If we're escaping, let's escape. I've got a place in Pasadena we can lay low."

"Go on," Mort said, making a shooing motion. "Get out before I change my mind." Realizing the stumbling block, he met Mriy's eyes and, with a jerk of his head, urged her out of the detective's path.

The five of them went their separate ways, the detective into the belly of the station, Mort and the rest left through the hole in the wall. Carl made a stop at the bloody mess of the detective on the floor to fish through the man's pockets.

"What are you waiting for?" Lloyd asked. "Come on!"

"Keys," Carl said, not looking up.

"I can take care of the handcuffs," Mort said. It wasn't the sort of thing that was worth lingering over. Letting the detective out was the starter's pistol of a race to freedom. If it weren't for the officers' inevitable confusion over a door, now magically held shut, they'd have already gotten to them. Once informed of the situation with the wall, it wouldn't be long before they came around the building.

"I imagine you can," Carl said. He fished a set of keys from the detective's pocket. Their merry jingle was incongruous with the dire situation. "But these keys will start his car." Carl's grin warmed Mort's heart. He was the reason for the highjinks of the *Mobius* and its crew. He made this shit *fun*.

Carl did manage to find the key to the handcuffs, and Detective Wallace's service revolver as well. The trigger seemed stiff, but he didn't dare pull it all the way for fear of firing it. Up close, it was a lot more complicated to reload than it looked in the old flatvids. There was a good chance he wouldn't be able to reload it without help from one of the locals—not that he'd thought to grab spare bullets.

"How are we going to know which car is Wallace's?" Lloyd asked. He didn't lower his voice, since they were a little past the point of a stealthy getaway.

"It was all squad cars out front," Carl reasoned. "Must be parked in the back."

There was indeed a general-use parking lot behind the station, filled with shiny new cars made to ancient blueprints. Like the rest of the colony though, it was a mish-mosh of eras, with new Model T's mixed in with early model Corvettes and Microbuses. Even Carl, whose historical education was limited to the entertainment industry, knew it was off.

"There are too many of them," Mriy said, punctuated by a grunt. It was weird hearing her voice coming out of Tanny's cousin Jimmy, but he'd seen stranger things result from Mort's magic. Best thing to do was to play along. But Jimmy or not, she'd taken a bullet in that jailbreak. Plenty of the blood all down her front was Detective Drake's, but enough of it wasn't that he was worried.

"You need a doctor?" Carl asked. It wasn't the side trip they needed just then. But the risk of arrest was worth it if Mriy was in bad shape.

"No."

She probably meant 'yes, but I'll be damned if we're going to one,' but Carl wasn't in the mood to argue. He studied the key in his hand, looking for a model badge, or a plate number, or any hint of what car it matched up with. All it had was an engraving of some sort of great cat. He wracked his brain for types of cars named after big cats. Tiger? Cheetah? Puma? Leopard?

"Can you tell what this is supposed to be?" Carl asked, holding the key chain toward Mriy.

"What am I? Your expert in all things—it's a jaguar," Mriy said. She was clutching a hand to her side.

"Mort, do something to stop her from bleeding," Carl said. "Lloyd, help me find a jag in this lot. I don't care what year or model. How many of them can there be?"

Officers poured through the back door of the station, but beat a hasty retreat as Mort raised a cage of flames to bar their path to the parking lot. Carl ducked between the rows of cars as shots rang out from the doorway.

"Found one!" Lloyd shouted over the roar of flames and gunfire. "Jaguar '63 S-Type."

Carl cursed his stiff knees as he struggled to run and crouch at the same time. He reached the car just as Mriy and Mort converged on it. He pressed the keys into Lloyd's hand. "Your world. You drive."

Lloyd shoved them back as if they were diseased. "Rhiannon drives. I haven't learned yet."

Carl pushed the keys toward Lloyd again. "And you think any of us know how?"

"I thought your whole family were retroverts at heart," Lloyd replied. "You must've seen it done in a holo. I walk to work. I take a cab to the ballpark. I'm scared shitless of driving one of these—"

"Fine," Carl snapped. "But strap in and hold on tight everyone. This could get interesting." They all piled into the vehicle, with Mort and Mriy in the back and Lloyd flying co-pilot.

The Jaguar started like a dream. Turning the key yielded a few cranks and the growl that only a petrol-burning engine can do justice. Carl revved the engine a few times, just enjoying the sound. Then he turned his attention to the stick shift. It was labeled simply: N-R-1-2-3-4.

A bullet punched a hole in the windshield between Carl and Lloyd. "Quit fooling with it and get us out of here," Lloyd snapped. It was the closest he'd heard to his boyfriend-in-law losing his temper. He was a real even guy, for a planetside historian.

"Sometime today would be nice," Mort said from the backseat.

"Some cover fire would be nice," Carl replied over his shoulder. "What're you waiting for?"

"You want to walk back to the ship?" Mort asked. "What're the odds this thing can handle me throwing lightning and fire around? I don't have a mule in my pocket to pull this thing if I kill it."

With a quick prayer generically addressed to the patron saint of car theft, Carl picked 'R' and hit the gas. Tires squealed, and a second later they shot backward in a cloud of rubber smoke. The wheel took some getting used to; it was close to a flight yoke, but not quite close enough, with multiple turns required to max out the car's turning radius. Stomping on the brakes threw the passengers sideways in their seats, then Carl shifted into '1' and switched to gas once more.

The Jaguar peeled out, and they jumped a curb onto the main road. It wasn't long before sirens wailed and blue lights shone in the rear-view mirror. It was hard to get a count of how many squad cars were following them, but Carl's best guess was "all of them."

"Great, now where are we headed?" Carl asked. "Tanny got the ship waiting somewhere nearby?"

"Nope," Mort replied. "It's back at the landing pen, with all the other spaceships."

Keeping one eye to their pursuers, Carl kept getting distracted by the image of Jimmy Rucker in his rearview. "Can you put Mriy back to normal without disabling the car? Fucking weird back there."

Mort gave a grunt in reply, and the illusion of Tanny's cousin faded. In its place was Mriy in a nun outfit. "What the hell, Mort? Just put her back to normal."

"This is how she snuck into Old Timey California," Mort replied. "Don't blame me."

"Sister Mriy, how you holding up back there? You're awfully quiet," Carl said. It wasn't that Mriy couldn't go long periods without hearing the sound of her own voice, but in these sorts of stressful, tactical situations, she usually had something to offer.

"You wouldn't... like the noises... I'd make right now," Mriy said between gasps. "I'll live. Leave me be."

"Roger that," Carl said. "Cat's down to seven lives, and no further updates until orbit."

"You have any bright ideas on how to get us to your ship?" Lloyd asked. "If I'd known there was no plan, I'd have stayed at the station and disavowed you."

"You're doing a nice job piloting this contraption," Mort said. "I really expected us to have to fight it out at the police depot."

Carl slipped the shifter from '1' to '2' to '4' and back to '1' again, with no change in the Jaguar's behavior. "Thanks, but this is an automatic. Someone didn't want to learn the hard way to drive, so they just dummied it up to look authentic. The pedal throttle is taking some getting used to, but the rest isn't that hard." There was another vehicle he'd recently learned to pilot. It wasn't sized for four, but it was a helluva lot closer than the *Mobius*. "Lloyd, can you get us to the highway that runs back toward the landing zone for off-world visitors?"

"Sure," Lloyd replied. "That'd be Route 66."

"Of course it would..."

Pilots are trained to go through a detailed and thorough preflight check prior to takeoff. Even if Carl had gone up in his Typhoon a thousand times, he would still check the most mundane and innocuous details before doing it again. Most of the time it was a precaution, double-checking the work of mechanics and maintenance staff aboard a carrier ship. Once in a while, it would catch something that wasn't *wrong*, but wasn't quite right either—things that fell under the category of personal pilot preference. But on rare occasion, it caught real problems, the sort of thing that grounded a fighter until someone took care of it. Maybe a sensor panel wasn't displaying. Maybe it was a fuel-cell bleeding energy. Maybe one of the life-support seals wasn't completely closing.

The Jaguar S-Type had a limited indicator console, and it hadn't occurred to Carl that any sort of pre-drive check would have been in order. Despite the half-dozen unfamiliar gauges, he might have noticed one needle that was pointing more toward 'E' than 'F' and puzzled out that it was low on fuel.

The Jaguar sputtered out in the middle of Route 66.

The convoy of police vehicles behind them had followed at a respectable distance, as if unsure how to handle a high-speed pursuit. Maybe they didn't know whether Carl had hostages. Or it could have been that they weren't eager to catch up with a wizard. Either way, that buffer zone of open highway between the Jaguar and the police were closing fast.

"Everyone out!" Carl ordered.

Car doors sprang open, and the four of them scrambled for the side of the road. Mort and Lloyd moved awkwardly in business suits, while Mriy struggled along with a bloody hand pressed to her side.

"What now, Carl?" Lloyd asked. "We're sitting ducks out here."

Carl looked down the road ahead of them. It was dark, moonlit, and a stretch he'd only seen once before from the other direction. Still, optimism seemed like the best course. "Probably only a couple klicks short of where I stashed the Squall. I'll go on ahead. You three hold them off."

"Hold them off?" Lloyd replied, a note of mania creeping into his voice. "We've got a half-empty revolver, and they've got the whole Anaheim police force. What've we got that—"

"Mort," Carl said, looking the old wizard square in the eye. "Keep the carnage to a minimum. Just keep them back while I get to the *Mobius*. There's going to be hell to pay for this. These cops see a starship, they'll put in a call to the ARGO garrison. That's when the real fun starts."

"Egads," Mort muttered. "We're depending on *you* to cover a mile of ground on foot. Maybe we should just surrender."

Mriy snickered, though she winced in pain with each movement. "Go. We trust you."

Carl gave a quick, informal salute and a wink. "Wish me luck!" He started out at a brisk jog in the direction he had last seen the Squall. Hopefully, it was closer than he was guessing.

As Carl disappeared into the gloom of night, Lloyd turned to Mort. The wail of sirens spread out as squad cars left the road to begin encircling them. The noise made conversation below a shout difficult, but Mriy's ears caught the muttered conversation that took place between them.

"Couldn't you just... you know... kill them all?" Lloyd asked, leaning close. "I've heard Rhiannon's stories. These pissant retrovert lawmen shouldn't be a threat to you."

Mort grunted and shrugged. "Carl asked nicely. These lads signed up to play cops and robbers, not to actually *be* cops. I can't imagine they get more than a few real crimes a year. This is a luxury resort more than a real ancient-Earth replica. It wouldn't be..." Mort scratched his chin a moment. "...sporting?"

At that moment, the encircling squad cars broke contact with the ground. They lifted awkwardly, wobbling as if pulled by the rood with invisible strings. Someone gave the order to open fire, and shots slapped harmlessly against an invisible barrier. More cars rose from the ground, each coming to a stop twenty meters or so in the air. But that didn't stop the panicked officers from firing.

"Cut that out!" Mort shouted at them. The replies that came back were unhelpful. Confused and frightened officers shouted instructions and orders, and the shots kept on coming. "Fine, then," he added in an undertone.

The cars began to spin, slowly at first, but increasingly fast until the squad cars had turned into the sort of carnival amusement ride that left weak-stomached passengers vomiting upon egress. There were a few screams at first, but those died away. Not as quickly as the shots stopped firing, however. The sirens fell silent as well, warped past functioning as magic broke down the local science.

Mort gave a satisfied nod. "That ought to hold them."

"How long can you keep it up?" Mriy asked.

Mort pursed his lips and frowned up at the squad cars. "I suppose I can leave them there until Carl gets back. It won't kill the poor saps. But I'll give them maybe half an hour; if Car's not back by then, I'll let them down to puke out everything from toenails to tongue. Doubt they'll be much trouble after that."

"They might radio for help," Lloyd said.

"The hell is a radio?" Mort asked.

Mriy strained to listen. "They are talking to someone at their headquarters, but there is no response. I think... you disabled those as well."

"Now we just wait. Anyone bring snacks?" Mort asked.

The Squall was right where Carl had left it. But he hadn't been the only one to discover it. Someone had adorned the hull with a peace symbol in dripping white spray-paint. In a panic, Carl checked for more substantive vandalism. All he found was a scrawled message on the far side, also in spray-paint, reading "Take me to your leader."

As he climbed into the cockpit, Carl worried that he might have missed something. Every pilot of a Typhoon was supposed to know the basics of how to maintain it; most of them could have been starship mechanics if they were inclined. But Carl had cheated his way through the academy testing, and his squad-mates had always covered for him after that. Something about the way all the trillions of little parts interacted just wouldn't settle into any form of sense in his head. He'd spent too much time with Mort as a kid and seen too much magic for science to seem scientific.

Knowing that there wasn't much he could do if he found anything, Carl skipped the pre-flight checks. Since there was no spray-paint, empty beer cans, or girls' underwear inside the Squall, he made the assumption that the teens who'd spray-painted it hadn't had the nerve to open it up. A few days on the side of a road shouldn't have hurt it any.

The engine hummed to life, and Carl grinned. He loved the music. He liked the style. But this backwater world was no place for a spacer. He hammered the throttle as soon as he was clear of the billboard he'd parked behind. On the trip out, he had kept low and slow to stay off sensors from the orbital nannies that enforced the retrovert lifestyle, finding and keeping out off-worlders and their tech toys. But now it was time to get shit done, and there was no hiding what he was planning to do next.

"Yo, Tanny," Carl said into the comm. "Tanny, answer me. Roddy? Pick up the comm. Need ya, buddy."

A few seconds later, the laaku mechanic came on the comm. "*Hey, Carl. Mort and Mriy went looking for you.*"

"They found me," Carl said. "I had to leave them back on the side of a highway, holding off the cops. I'm coming in hot."

"Why is it never a nice, leisurely departure?" Roddy said. "Why's everyplace we leave gotta involve the word 'flee' or

'escape'? You ever think I might be doing maintenance on the engines, or something?"

"That's why I keep the fridge well stocked," Carl replied. "To keep you from being ambitious and proactive. Have the cargo bay open and engines fired up. I'll take the helm, but I want you to get us off the ground before I get up there."

"That much of a hurry, huh?"

"That much of a hurry. We just pulled the fire alarm, and ARGO's going to come down on us before too long. Those retrovert cops aren't the problem, it's who they'll call for backup."

"I'm on it."

Carl closed the comm and opened a new one. It took him a moment to remember the comm ID, since it wasn't programmed into the Squall. "Hailing. Lost little girl, come in." When there was no response, he repeated the message, and then a third time before he got a response.

"Jesus, Carl," Rhiannon said. "You ever stop to think I might have company over? It's not cool for me to be using this thing planetside. Quit being such a square, and patch it through the phone."

"Wait! Don't hang up!" Carl said. "This is serious. Lloyd, Mort, and Mriy are in trouble. I'm rushing back to the *Mobius* to go pick them up."

"Sounds like a bad scene," Rhiannon said. "Lay it on me."

"Mort broke me out of jail while Lloyd was there," Carl said. "It got all... well, like everything I do. Lloyd came along instead of playing dumb, so he's caught up in this."

"No way!" Rhiannon said. "Lloyd wouldn't get himself tagged. He's a total dork; wears his suit on the inside, you know?"

"Listen to me," Carl said. "Shit flows downhill from this.

We're taking Lloyd with us and bugging out. Making tracks. Fleeing the scene? You dig, Sis?"

"*Fuck.*" She got the idea, which was good, because Carl was running out of period-authentic lingo to use on her.

"If you want to join us, have anything you want to bring with you in the car when I get there."

"Where do I meet you?" Rhiannon asked. "How soon? Oh, and fuck you, Carl."

"Yeah, fuck me," Carl agreed. "But just be in the driveway in..." Carl checked his sensors and did some guessing. "Let's say twenty minutes."

Carl sprinted through the *Mobius*, which was in the air before he set the Squall down in the cargo bay. As the ramp closed behind him, he could see that Roddy was bringing it about, setting in a course for the way he'd just come. He skidded to a halt and slammed into the co-pilot's seat.

"Move over," he ordered Roddy.

"Always a treat with you around," Roddy said, easing back on the throttle before leaving the controls momentarily unattended.

Carl slid into the pilot's chair as Roddy moved into the co-pilot's. "Well, shit happens."

"It's all your fault, you know," Roddy said. "*All* your fault. From being here in the first place, to Harmony Bay shitting bricks over your crash-and-burn at the race, to Phabian Investigative Services giving us the scan-job."

"Well, add ruining my sister's life to the list," Carl said. "We're swinging by Rhiannon's place after we grab everyone else. Where's Tanny?"

"She and Esper took a transport ship," Roddy said. "They couldn't wait for you to get back before they went after Kubu."

"Just the two of them?" Carl said. "Shit."

"That's your fault, too, I guess."

Carl had to ponder that one a moment before it sank in. Why would the two of them running off get dumped in *his* lap? It sounded more like Tanny couldn't keep it together long enough to form a proper rescue plan. "It was Mort, wasn't it?"

"Yeah, the big guy wouldn't drop the *Mobius* astral without you on board," Roddy said. "Not that Tanny cared about leaving you on Peractorum until we got back."

"We'll have a word about that later," Carl promised. Tanny was getting out of hand. Carl not being on the ship sort of put her in charge, but it didn't make the *Mobius* hers to run off with and leave him stranded. "Looks like I owe Mort one, huh?"

Roddy made a rude noise of flapping lips. "We *all* owe that crusty old bastard more than we could ever pay back."

"Still..."

"Yeah," Roddy agreed. "I know. Hey, where'd you leave the jail breakers?"

"Just off Route 66," Carl replied.

Roddy rolled his eyes. "You nostalgic fuckers. A whole colony without one original idea in it."

While the *Mobius* was nowhere near as agile at the Squall parked in its belly, in a straight line through atmosphere, it was nearly as fast. But the comforting bulk and the lack of a panoramic view through the canopy made the return trip feel more relaxing. An overlay holo-display cast the nighttime landscape in easily viewed shades of green, making navigation a simple matter of backtracking the Squall's course, plus a bit of rounding error for the part he took on foot.

When he spotted the police cars floating in mid-air, Carl slammed on the thrust reversers and brought the *Mobius* to a halt. Mort had taken the defensive posture down at ground level a bit farther than Carl had anticipated. This wasn't just going to make the local papers. They were going to have every investigative branch in ARGO here pretty soon, maybe even someone from the Convocation. Magic like that didn't go unnoticed on civilized worlds, even when those worlds tried their damnedest not to seem civilized.

"Roddy, grab a seat in the turret and cover them," Carl said. "Fire a few warning shots."

"Are you nuts?" Roddy asked. "We can't just—"

"Yes," Carl snapped. "I am. We're putting astral between us and ARGO for a while after this. A lot of it. Now go! And open the cargo bay while you're at it."

Carl kept them on the outskirts of what he guessed might be the range of Mort's fuckery when it came to the laws of physics. For having known the wizard twenty-something years, it was still guesswork figuring out how far and how badly he could screw with technology.

Roddy's first volley kicked up huge plumes of dust in the dry dirt fields on the side of the road. The greenish bolts of plasma hadn't flown quite straight, taking a curved path to the ground, but Roddy had given the squad cars a wide berth when he fired. After a second blast, the cars drifted to the ground. When they'd settled onto their own suspensions, Carl backed the *Mobius* up to the three fugitives, cargo ramp first.

"*We're... aboard,*" Mriy grunted on the comm a moment later. She sounded bad. But Mriy was tough. If she hadn't died of her wounds by now, she ought to be able to recover. Maybe once they picked up Esper, she could do something to help.

Carl trusted that Mriy had already hit the controls for the

ramp. He gained altitude and put the shields up—just in case a bullet got lucky.

"We can't leave without Rhiannon," Lloyd's voice came over the comm.

Carl gave a rueful smile. Not a bad guy, Lloyd. Might do a good job looking after his sister. "Already on the way. Called ahead. She's packing as we speak."

The nav computer had updated with local maps. It recognized the address 413 Mapleview Terrace and showed Carl a course and an ETA of two minutes—God, were starships convenient. A scan off the orbital comm chatter didn't show up with anything unusual, but it was scant comfort. Back when they had Chip, he'd have been listening in on encrypted-law enforcement channels. But just about anything could be on its way to Peractorum through astral and the *Mobius* wouldn't know until it was too late.

Mapleview Terrace was the same bland, cookie-cutter happy factory that every other residential zone in the 'burbs seemed to be. It was just like Mom and Dad's old place in San Jose, back during the brief period when they'd lived here. Ranch floor plan, white picket fence, postage stamp yard with vibrant green grass. It was easy to pick out Rhiannon's place, because it was the only one with a woman in an orange dress frantically stuffing suitcases into a Camero.

The *Mobius* landed only briefly. It was just long enough for Rhiannon to drive a '68 Camero replica into the cargo hold and park it beside the Squall. Carl stayed up in the cockpit, dreading the fallout from his sister's unplanned addition to the passenger manifest. Hopefully, if Lloyd were any sort of boyfriend, he'd calm her down before the subject of fratricide came up.

Carl headed for space.

Tanny being Tanny, she had left a detailed itinerary of the

rescue mission, along with three alternate rendezvous points for afterward, and a comm ID to get in touch with her anonymously if things went sideways. But with Mort aboard, Carl figured there was a chance they might even head her off before she did anything stupid on her own.

Esper wasn't going to be nearly enough backup for a rescue.

There were times when Esper seemed like her old self. At the cafeteria on board the *Milky Waltz*, she'd ordered herbal tea and chocolate cake for breakfast. They'd watched *Love Letter Dynasty* together in their shared berth, weeping over Laurie and Jackson's tragic affair while drinking sweetened wine. Without the guys around, it had been like a vacation.

And then there were times when she seemed distant, shouldering her way through crowds and glowering at overly talkative servers. Tanny wanted to talk to her about it, but there was the mission to consider. If it took Esper letting her mind wander into Mort's dreams to turn her into the soldier she needed to be... for a few days that would have to do.

But that trip was behind them now. They had arrived on Nythy, the vowel-free laaku colony world where Inviu of Chapath had set up her refuge. It was an unauthorized terraformed world, not part of ARGO's master plan to fully colonize the galaxy. Its gravity was 1.1 of Earth's, which put it 5% over the threshold for sanctioned habitation. Of course, after a while planetside, most people didn't notice the difference, and with an illegally terraformed atmosphere and imported wildlife, Nythy made for decent living.

"I feel like an idiot in this getup," Tanny whispered. "How

did I let you talk me into this?" The sleeves of her tunic were baggy, and she had her hands stuffed inside opposing sleeves, mimicking Esper's posture.

"If we want Kubu free and clear, we need to get in without them knowing who's coming," Esper said. "I don't think your phony IDs were going to do the trick."

"And *your* phony wizard trick will?" Tanny asked. "At least you could have let me know before I paid for the IDs."

"You should have told me about it, and I would have stopped you," Esper replied. "And Mort and I have already pulled this trick. I'm no Mort, but I think I can pass you off as an apprentice."

"You think..." Tanny muttered. "I can't even remember the last time I wore a skirt. I must look ridiculous."

"It's January 9th, 2561," Esper said. "Next time I make you wear one, you'll know. Besides, you look cute in a skirt. And black is *definitely* your color."

They left the starport on foot, but soon found a communal transport heading for the Duploth region, which was their destination. There wasn't much infrastructure, just a concrete pad and a service desk—pay at one, wait near the other. It was half an hour until the next shuttle. Tanny and Esper sat down on a bench by the pad and waited.

"I'd feel better if we had a datapac with us," Tanny said. "Shipping our tech to Keesha Bell seems like cutting our own throats."

"She'll hold onto it for us," Esper replied. The calm assurance in her voice was new as of the past few days. She didn't hedge and suggest and qualify, she just said things like she meant them. "Besides, to get in without raising a ruckus, we need to stay in character."

"And without a blaster, you think I won't end up killing Inviu," Tanny reasoned.

"Maybe," Esper said. "But I bet if you really, *really* deep in your heart want to, you could kill her with your bare hands. No blaster just means you can't do it without thinking."

Tanny couldn't take it any longer. "What's gotten into you? Mort can't be having this much effect on you in a couple nights. You haven't even gone into his head since we've been... wait, you haven't, right?"

"No," Esper said. "And it's been weird waking up in modern times multiple days in a row. But I don't know, maybe I'm just growing up. I ran away to the One Church for protection and for answers. I got some of one and not nearly enough of the other. Mort's got answers. I don't like a lot of them, but he offers them up anyway. They're better answers than I had, at least."

"So Mort's put you off the One Church now?" Tanny asked. "Jesus, he's one cold-hearted bastard. Take away solace in life and the comfort of the next..."

"No, just a more complete picture," Esper said. "He's studied history like you wouldn't believe. The scriptures, the heresies, the histories that get stuffed in a closet because they don't agree with 'popular' history. He's got copies in his head, and I've read a bunch of them. It helps to see past the politics and the secular power grabs to the divinity beneath. Mortal men acting on behalf of God with real magic, performing miracles with His gifts. Atrocities in His name and in defiance of His laws. Humanity is shit, a lot of the time."

"There!" Tanny said. "That! You didn't used to curse like that."

Esper just shrugged. "I used to think there was something inherently wrong with certain words," she said. "I was brought up that way. But a lot of how I was raised was fucked up. Fucked. Fucking fucked the fuck up. Am I supposed to go tell a priest I said that? Half of them sin daily anyway. Does he have God's ear any more than I do? Is He not listening to me *right now*? There's nothing in the Ten Commandments about vocabulary; English wasn't even around back then."

"I can see you've had some time on your hands," Tanny muttered. She started to check her datapad for the dozenth time before remembering yet again that it was in a shipping crate en route to Champlain VI.

"A lot of the confusion comes from translations," Esper continued. A dam had burst, and all the things she'd been keeping silent on had flooded forth. Tanny now regretted poking holes in that dam. "A lot of other races that heard God's word kept simpler versions. Ten was a lot of commandments, possibly because humanity—as I mentioned—has been pretty shitty over the years. But the tesuds have a single commandment: '*In all actions, seek to lessen suffering.*' It's such a catch-all. So simple, but so hard to wrap your head around."

"How do you quantify suffering?" Tanny asked. "Sounds like a great way to rationalize theft from the rich."

"Ah," Esper said with a grin. "But if they were pious, they'd have used the money to reduce suffering already. Still, the theory has its flaws. Temporal ignorance of the greater suffering in the world and worlds beyond is one of the key theological topics in the tesuds' equivalent of the One Church."

Tanny let Esper ramble on. It was nice that Mort was broadening Esper's horizons beyond fire-and-brimstone morality, but Tanny had come to terms with the lack of a caring god a long time ago. She's seen too much—hopefully more suffering than Esper would ever know about. There very possibly was a god, but he didn't give a counterfeit terra about humanity.

...otherwise he might have sent that shuttle along just a

little ahead of schedule.

Under the guise of prospective donors from the Convocation, Tanny and Esper had no trouble arranging a tour at the Duploth Refuge for Sentient and Displaced Species. They were met at the shuttle depot by a young laaku in a green and white uniform. He was piloting a blocky, weather-worn cargo shuttle that looked like it had seen heavy use outdoors.

"Welcome to Duploth," he said, extending a hand. Tanny and Esper each removed a hand from their sleeves to shake with and returned to their Convocation-approved 'I'm not here to do magic' poses. "I'm Chimjo of Nederhal, park ranger for the reserve. Climb aboard."

The interior of the shuttle had a barnyard odor, reeking of animal sweat and rich soil. The seats were old leather, worn and cracked, with harness-style straps for the occupants. Tanny strapped herself in as soon as she sat down; Esper never removed her hands from her sleeves as she took her seat. Out of the corner of her eye, Tanny kept watch to see how Esper handled keeping her seat on a bucket of bolts that probably didn't have its own gravity generator—hence the restraints.

But as the shuttle rose, Esper rocked with the ship's motion and kept herself steady as the straps strained to hold Tanny tightly in place. "Hold on. This is a short ride, but maybe not a smooth one," Chimjo said from the cockpit. Despite being able to hear him a bit, speakers in the passenger section relayed his voice with an annoying audio parallax.

The trip was, as promised, both short and rough. Tanny's shoulders ached when she unfastened her harness, and she caught a sly smile from Esper as she rubbed the spot where the straps had dug in. Their landing spot was a smaller version of the concrete slab outside the starport, with the service desk replaced by a supply shed. Chimjo met them on the pad and escorted them to a ground vehicle with no visible means of locomotion.

"Well, here you have it, one of the largest privately funded, POGOFAFEP-approved refuges in the galaxy," Chimjo said, waving a hand across their field of view as he started the vehicle. It hummed forward with far less panache than the petrol-burners back in New Cali, crawling along the ground.

"POGOFAFEP?" Esper asked before Tanny could.

"The Phabian Organization for Galactic Ocean Flora and Fauna Extinction Protection," Chimjo said. "Sorry, not being laaku, I shouldn't have assumed you knew. They're the galaxy's leading authority on the care and nurturing of at-risk species."

"I see," Esper said.

"So what are you going to show us?" Tanny asked. It was one thing to play the tourist and potential donor, but she didn't want to linger around this place all day.

"Well, for starters, we're headed to the forest section," Chimjo replied. "We've got fifty-three species of avian life, as well as a number of—"

"Do you have any megafauna?" Esper asked. "I was on Vi Tik Naa once, and they had this great safari that—"

"We don't approve of that place around here," Chimjo said with an ominous note in his voice. "That's a hunting world. Damn shame what goes on out there beyond ARGO."

"Wouldn't it be nice if someone brought those big, wonderful creatures somewhere safe?" Esper asked sweetly. "You don't have any big, ancient creatures around here, do you?"

"Ancient?" Chimjo said. "Wouldn't say ancient, but then again, you're human, so you drove all sorts of creatures extinct."

"A little before our time," Tanny mumbled.

"We do have some pretty big creatures around here," Chimjo said. "We've got a mammoth clan in the Northwest part of the reserve. They keep to themselves mostly, and find their own food, but they know me and don't mind me being around. Not sure that's the best place to go looking though."

"What else've you got?" Tanny asked.

Chimjo sighed. She could tell that he believed in this place and must have thought they were gawking clods. If it weren't for the promise of a donation to fund the reserve, he'd probably have kicked them out of the vehicle to walk back to the shuttle pad. "We've got a bear/tiger hybrid rescued from a genetics lab, but she's skittish around new people—can't say I blame her. There's also a long-beaked condor with a nest not far from here. Last of his kind as far as we know; rescued him from the Sarfeist Cluster. And there's a sentient canid from Poltid, fresh in from a private collector—still just a kid, really."

"Sentient?" Esper said with a grin. "Ooh, can we meet him?"

It was a good thing she spoke up quickly, because Tanny was about ready to grab the little monkey by the throat and wring Kubu's location out of him.

Chimjo checked a chrono on the vehicle's control console. "Well... not right now. It's lesson time. Mrs. Inviu takes a particular interest in rescued sentients. They get proper schooling, tailored to their intellectual development needs."

Esper cast Tanny a speculative glance. Damn her! Yes, Tanny needed to come up with something to teach Kubu. He *did* need some sort of education, and 'living aboard a starship' wasn't enough on its own. He'd learn about heists and engine maintenance and a million different plots to holovids, but not the ABCs and arithmetic that were the foundation of literacy and productive society.

"Maybe afterward?" Esper asked.

Chimjo lifted his cap and scratched the back of his head—which fortunately left two hands for driving—before answering. "We'll see. Maybe. That's all I can promise."

"What's that building over there?" Tanny asked. A structure of white and silver glinted on the horizon.

"You've got good eyes," Chimjo remarked. "That's the main house. Anything that prefers an indoor sleeping situation gets a room or stable or whatever they need."

"Is that where Kubu is?" Esper asked.

Chimjo cut the throttle and the vehicle came to an abrupt halt. Twisting around in the seat, he confronted the two would-be wizards. "Who the hell are you? I never mentioned Kubu's name."

Tanny shot a hand out and grabbed Chimjo by his collar. "I'm his Mommy."

Chimjo grabbed Tanny's wrist with his upper hands and brought his lower two to bear against her chest. "Lemme go, you crazy ape!" He was startlingly strong for his size, threatening to tear the fabric of his own uniform to free himself from Tanny's grasp.

But Tanny only had one hand occupied. With the other, she gave Chimjo a swift cuff to the side of the head. His struggles abated momentarily, but when his dizziness passed, he resumed his efforts to break free. With all the patience she could muster, Tanny measured out a slightly stiffer blow and struck the laaku ranger again. During his daze, she shook him, dislodging his feet from her chest.

"I won't help you... kidnap him," Chimjo mumbled with his head lolling forward.

"We're not kidnapping him," Esper said. "We're here to rescue him. If he doesn't want to come, we won't force him."

"Inviu's... legal guardian."

Tanny lifted Chimjo's chin so he was looking her in the eye. "We are—to put it mildly—not concerned about legalities."

"I need that on a coffee mug," Esper muttered.

"We're here to get Kubu back where he belongs," Tanny said. "With the people who rescued him and who he trusts. I didn't save him from one zoo to put him into another one, even if it's a little nicer."

"Can't keep him on a starship," Chimjo said. "No place for... big animal like that."

"Not your problem," Tanny said. "Now, I've got Convocation backup here, but I don't need this to get any more violent than it's already been. We'll be gone and you'll never see any of the three of us ever again."

"Not... help you."

"Dammit!" Tanny shouted into the limp laaku's face. "Yes you will, or you'll regret it. If I have to, I'll—"

"Were you friends with Kubu?" Esper asked.

"Huh?"

"Does Kubu like you?" Esper asked. "Have you been kind to him?" She lowered her voice. "I'll know if you're lying."

"Kubu's a good boy," Chimjo said. "I think he likes everybody. I take him hunting... find bunnies."

"Let him go," Esper ordered. It was odd hearing an order from those lips. But Tanny knew she meant it and wasn't hearing arguments against it. She set the laaku on the seat of the vehicle and loosened her grip until he stood on his own, leaning heavily against the seat back.

"Don't do this," Chimjo said. "He's better off here. Mrs. Inviu can take proper care—"

"Get out," Tanny told him. "If you're not helping us, fine. Since you haven't done anything to Kubu, we'll let you go. But we're taking this... whatever you call this thing. And if you go calling for help, you're just going to get a lot of people hurt. Maybe us, too. Maybe Kubu. But definitely a lot of your coworkers, and I'll make *sure* one of them is *you*. Got it, four-hands?"

"Got it," Chimjo said, stumbling out of the vehicle.

"That was uncalled for," Esper said as they sped off with Tanny at the controls. Despite its odd appearance, efficient laaku design had left the vehicle starkly simple to operate.

"Hm?" Tanny grunted.

"Calling him four-hands," Esper said. "I mean, he *has* four of them, but you were deriding him for it. Would you have called him that if Roddy were here?"

"In a heartbeat," Tanny said. They were bouncing along uneven terrain in a machine of a vehicular breed she'd never heard of. It wasn't the time to get cutesy-fuzzy over word choice. "Roddy knows his up from down. It's not personal."

Esper slid her hands into her sleeves and gave a cautious nod. "Let's keep that idea at the fore. This is a rescue, not a vendetta. And I *mean* that."

For the first time since they'd been on this mission, Tanny realized that she might not be in charge of it.

The main structure of the Duploth Refuge was larger than Tanny had guessed from a distance. It didn't appear to be residential-grade building materials, either. It had the look of a modular colony for non-atmospheric worlds, or ones with toxic air. The only saving grace appeared to be the front door, which had a welcoming, business-like appearance, with glass double-doors and a sign above, lettered in some laaku language Tanny couldn't read. She assumed that it was a welcome of some sort.

The strange, crawling vehicle halted out front as Tanny cut power to the throttle. She vaulted over the side and hustled up to the door, with Esper following suit. "Shit, camera!" she snapped, turning away from the black glass dome in the corner by the door.

"Well, she's not going to wonder for long who came for Kubu anyway," Esper said. "Not like she can't scan the omni for your service record and get an image that way. Kubu's only got so many mommies."

Tanny tried the door, but the handle wouldn't budge. Set into the white steel wall was an input panel, with a screen that was also displaying laaku script. "English," she said, and the screen complied. It asked her to identify herself and offered voice, retinal, DNA, and password validation as options.

"Where's the option for none of the above?" Esper asked, peering over Tanny's shoulder. "Oh, wait..." She gently guided Tanny out of her way, then mashed a hand against the screen. The image seen around that slender hand went haywire, twisting, then flickering, then blank.

"Nice," Tanny said. She heaved on the door handle, but it still wouldn't open. "Bullshit! Fail secure? What kind of place is this? They lose power, everyone's trapped inside."

"Unless they've got a wizard," Esper said. Once again, she pushed her way past Tanny, this time taking custody of the door handle. The 50-kilo slip of a woman set her feet, gritted her teeth, and pulled.

Nothing happened.

"Hold on," Esper said through gritted teeth. She put a foot against one door while pulling on the handle of the other.

Still, nothing happened.

"I think you need to try your next trick," Tanny said. "And make it quick, we must've gotten someone's attention in there by now."

"This door is... rather insistent that it's actually closed," Esper said. "I'm having a *very* hard time convincing it otherwise. I think Inviu might have coached it on what to do against wizards." There was sweat beading on her forehead, but no sign of the door giving so much as a millimeter to show for it.

"If only I had a blaster," Tanny grumbled. It wasn't an efficient way to get through a door, not at the output power of a hand-held. But it was a helluva lot better than muscle power, even magically juiced muscle power. "Hold up a minute. Don't herniate yourself."

Tanny ran back for the crawler and hopped into the driver's seat. It was the most awkward vehicle she could remember using, but it seemed to have good traction. She swung it around and backed it up the front steps. Catching on to what Tanny was planning, Esper scrambled out of the way before the crawler hit the doors. They protested briefly, bulging inward before buckling under the strain. The glass didn't shatter, just bent and crumpled like steel. It was a wizarding trick, same as Mort has done years ago for all the glass aboard the *Mobius*. It was still weird to look at the results.

Esper climbed through the open cabin of the crawler to follow Tanny into the building. The halls were stark white, scrubbed spotless, and serenely lit. Flatvid screens showed footage promoting the work of the refuge, with laaku caretakers interacting with a variety of rare and exotic creatures. It brought back memories of the Gologlex Menagerie, which helped steel her resolve.

"Hold it right there!" a laaku voice shouted. It had only been a matter of time, she supposed. They hadn't been quick, or stealthy, or the least bit subtle in their entrance. If she'd proposed that sort of breach in tactical school, she'd have flunked the course.

Two laaku in park ranger uniforms like Chimjo's had their heads poking out from a side corridor, rifles aimed at Tanny and Esper. Seconds later, another pair emerged from a corridor farther down, advancing slowly with their rifles trained on the two intruders.

"Easy boys," Tanny said, raising her hands. "We're unarmed."

"Put down your weapons," Esper ordered. She raised a single hand, not in surrender. An image formed in the palm of that hand, as if held there by the loose grip of her outstretched fingers. It was the sigil of the Convocation, same as Mort used when he wanted to bully someone without using actual magic —which was rare. "This is Convocation business. Stand aside and you won't be harmed." To Tanny's shock, Esper started down the corridor right for them, as if they were just holo images of actual guards.

But they hesitated. Tanny noticed one of the laaku down the hall take a tentative step back. Another poked around the corner, angling his weapon to point away from her.

"My business is with Inviu of Chapath. Where can I find her?" Esper asked. Tanny had never understood magic, not beyond what she'd seen it do with her own eyes. Was it possible that this *was* Mort, or a fragment of Mort that had been deposited in Esper's brain? Had he cross-pollinated with her? Or had Esper really changed so much in a few short days.

A few long days, Tanny amended. Something Esper had said on the transport ship en route came back to her. In a month's time, she'd be twice as old as Tanny. She would have spent more of her perceived life in Mort's dreamland than in the real world.

"Bring her here!" Esper snapped when none of the rangers

seemed inclined to supply information on their employer's whereabouts. "And put those ridiculous toys away before you hurt someone."

"They're set on stun," one of the rangers said by way of apology. "We don't fire lethal weapons in the refuge."

"Good," Esper said. "Now find Inviu, and bring her to me."

"Inviu is right here," a new voice said. Tanny recognized it from the background of the comm Kubu had managed to send her shortly after his capture. The laaku woman who stepped into the corridor didn't look like any sort of wizard. But then again, Mort didn't either, most of the time. She was dressed in coveralls stained with dirt around the ankles and wore a pair of old-fashioned spectacles. She tucked a pair of gardening gloves into a pocket. "What business does the Convocation have here? Since when do you people bother with... It's *you*!" Inviu looked squarely at Tanny as she said it. "These aren't wizards. These are the poachers who stole Kubu! And they're here to do it again. Detain them."

The first shot missed Esper by the finger's width, a blue energy that dissipated as soon as it struck steel. She pushed off against the nearest wall, thrusting herself out of the line of fire, then kicked off the far wall like a springboard. As she was about to slam into the pair of laaku at the corner, they both got their rifles aimed center-of-mass at her. But nothing fired. Esper must have fouled the tech that the rifles relied upon.

Tanny wasn't about to allow Esper to face the laaku all by herself. She rushed forward, yelling incoherently to draw attention and sow panic. The two laaku at the end of the hall retreated for cover, firing poorly aimed shots in the hope of slowing her. They didn't. Tanny's target wasn't the two retreating rangers, nor the two that Esper was pummeling. She was after Inviu, and the laaku woman knew it.

Inviu fled, hurtling down the corridor on all fours. Even with her pharmaceutically enhanced muscles, Tanny couldn't match a healthy laaku in a sprint. But that didn't stop her from pursuing. She saw Inviu disappear through a side door, and seconds later, Tanny threw it open and barged through. She was just in time to see Inviu disappear around a corner and headed off after her. This place wasn't big enough for the laaku kidnapper to hide.

Tanny rounded the next bend and froze in place. She hadn't intended to. But Inviu stood in the next room, arms crossed, with a smug look on her face. Try as she might, Tanny couldn't budge a muscle.

"Kubu, come here," Inviu said in a soft voice. "Look who's here."

Kubu peeked through an open door at the far end of the room. Good God, he'd grown huge. He must have put on thirty kilos since she'd last seen him. And he was wearing clothes—some sort of kiddie outfit, grossly oversized. "Mommy?" Kubu asked. "MOMMY!" He bounded across the room, and Tanny felt a moment's panic as she was unable to brace herself for the affectionate onslaught. The canid slammed into her like a huge sack of furry meat (which she supposed he was). He licked her face, tail wagging furiously. "Oh, Mommy, Mommy, Mommy. Kubu missed you."

"I don't love you," Tanny said, shocked to hear the words come from her own mouth, which moved of its own accord.

"Mommy?" Kubu backed a step away. His tail still wagged, but more slowly.

"I'm here to steal you back, because you belong to me," Tanny heard herself say. She wanted to scream that it wasn't true, that she *did* love Kubu, and that Inviu was forcing her to say these things.

"You see, Kubu?" Inviu asked, strolling up and laying a

hand on the back of Kubu's neck. She had to reach up to manage. "She was lying to you all that time. She wasn't going to take good care of you like I do. But my magic stopped her, kept you safe. I'll always keep you safe."

Kubu whined and hung his head, ears folded back. "Mommy? Why?"

"Because Inviu is a witch," Esper said from somewhere behind Tanny, out of her field of vision. "She's not really saying those things, Kubu. It's a trick."

"Esper!" Kubu said. He started toward her with the same enthusiasm he'd initially shown Tanny, but Inviu stopped him in his tracks.

"Stop!" Inviu commanded, then turned her attention to Esper. "So... you actually *are* some sort of wizard. But you're not here on behalf of the Convocation, are you? This is a kidnapping, plain and simple."

"Yeah," Esper replied. "I guess when *you* kidnap someone, you get a lot more lawyers involved. We don't go to that sort of trouble. Kubu's family, and we look after family ourselves." As Esper came into Tanny's peripheral vision, she noticed that Esper had brought one of the stun rifles along. She took aim at Inviu. "Now let them go. We're leaving, and it only gets uglier from here if you try to stop us."

As Esper inched forward, aiming the stun rifle at Inviu, the laaku woman scoffed. "You think you can bluff me? That thing won't fire. If your magic hadn't already fouled it, mine would." Esper froze awkwardly, mid-step.

But the magical halting was broken a split-second later. "Not on me, you don't," Esper warned. "And as for this thing?" She switched her grip, taking her finger off the trigger and grabbing the rifle by the barrel in both hands. "It's still three kilos of polymer composite." With that, she swung the rifle at Inviu like a club. The laaku wizard barely had time to dive out of the way. Esper swung again, and Inviu leapt onto a desk, which Esper promptly kicked out from under her.

Tanny felt the hold on her loosen. Esper must have been distracting Inviu to the point where she couldn't maintain her iron hold on Tanny's muscles.

"Kubu, help me!" Inviu ordered, scampering away from Esper, who cut off her path to the door before she could escape.

Tanny couldn't believe the stones on this laaku woman, expecting Kubu to help *her* after Esper revealed the lies Inviu had forced out of her mouth. He might be a bit naive, but Kubu wasn't stupid. But to her horror, Kubu started moving toward Esper, and it didn't look friendly.

"Esper," Tanny managed to say, fighting against Inviu's weakened control of her body. "Look out."

As soon as Esper snapped her head around, Inviu darted for the door. Kubu lurched forward like a stiff-legged puppet. Tanny didn't care how strong she'd gotten, Esper could punch Kubu until she broke every bone in her hand and not phase him. He closed in on her.

"Run," Tanny grunted out.

"Kubu..." Esper said, spreading her arms. "It's OK. I'm your friend. Inviu can't do this to you. She can't make you do things you don't like." Kubu kept approaching her. "You are Kubu. You are your own person. Believe that!"

Kubu kept plodding toward her, but slowed. Esper didn't back away. If Tanny didn't do something, he was going to crush Esper flat. She strained against the invisible bonds holding her, but it was as if she were buried in sand. All she could do was twitch a few millimeters and no farther.

"I believe in you, Kubu," Esper repeated. She reached out a hand and placed it on the bridge of Kubu's nose. He stopped.

A tense moment passed, then Kubu shrugged Esper's hand off his nose and licked her.

Tanny felt herself break free all at once. She stumbled as straining muscles all sprang loose without warning. Kubu turned and reached her in a single bound. "Mommy! Oh, Mommy, Kubu missed you!"

With a wellspring of tears, Tanny threw her arms around Kubu. "I missed you, too." She sniffed and pulled away. "But we still have to stop Inviu, or we'll never—"

"No," Esper said.

"But we can't just let her get away with—"

"NO."

Kubu followed the argument, looking from Tanny to Esper and back again as they argued. "What are we 'NO' about?"

"We've got Kubu," Esper said. "That's all we came for. We've got to get out of here before someone calls for bigger help than a few park rangers with science rifles." Tanny couldn't help noting Mort's term for technological weaponry.

"But she'll—"

"NO!" Esper shouted. "This is why Mort sent me. This isn't an assassination; it's a rescue. Come on, Kubu, we have a thingy out front that drives like a snake or a snail or something. It'll be fun."

Kubu nodded. "Mommy, come with Esper and Kubu?"

Tanny took a slow, shuddering breath. "Yeah, OK." The tactical training ingrained deep down in her said that leaving Inviu loose was a mistake, that she'd come after them sooner or later—maybe as soon as they exited the building. But she had Kubu back, and until they were safely off-world, that was a tenuous thing. "Let's go."

The plans Mort had passed along had included an inventory of ships that Inviu of Chapath kept on site for various uses. Most were for cargo and large animal transport, dependent on larger carrier ships or astral gates for interstellar travel. But one was a *Gaedri*-class low-end luxury transport with its own astral drive. That was going to be their ticket off-world.

As Tanny piloted the crawler toward Inviu's landing pad, a glow of main engine thrusters caught her attention. "Shit," she muttered.

Esper looked up to the sky; Kubu looked to the ground. "Where?" he asked.

"What was that?" Esper asked, following Tanny's gaze.

"Pretty sure that was our ride," she replied. "Inviu must have bolted straight for it when she ran. I would have thought she'd put up more fight for her refuge than that."

"It explains why you and Kubu were able to break free," Esper said. "I didn't *think* that was anything I did, but it was hard to be sure. Magic's not the easiest thing in the world to keep track of."

"Well, nothing to do but keep going," Tanny said. "Worst case, we steal a sub-orbital and find our way to a starport."

Esper snorted. "Since when are *you* the optimist? I can think of loads of cases worse than that."

The landing pad was all but deserted. If Inviu had more ships there earlier in the day, her workforce had already used them to evacuate the area. All that was left was a touring ship—one of the transparent-bottomed craft meant for fly-overs of scenic landscapes.

"Can you fly it?" Esper asked, laying a hand on the hull.

Tanny walked around the ship, a foreboding sense that someone was on the way to arrest them gnawing at her. "Maybe. It's only got one engine right now—other one's half taken apart—but I don't see any damage. It looks like it might be spaceworthy."

"That's all we need right now," Esper said. "Get in."

The three of them piled inside, and Tanny took the pilot's seat. She adjusted the chair to human anatomy as best she could, but it was clearly intended for a laaku pilot. A quick pre-flight check confirmed the dead engine (half its parts were on the concrete outside), but otherwise the ship looked functional. One red indicator on the sensor panel caught her attention. "Strap in, we've got company coming." The target ID function on the little tour ship was shit; but the incoming ship was large—at least a patrol ship. "I don't know how much evasive maneuvering we can do with this, but maybe if I get us to the mountains—"

"Head to orbit," Esper said.

"This thing has no star-drive," Tanny argued. "They'll have us dead to rights."

"Leave atmosphere, and call in our surrender," Esper said. "That'll buy me time to drop us astral." Whether Tanny was meant to hear the last part or not, she did, but Esper added, in an undertone, "Plus time to pray."

Tanny swore under her breath and plotted a trajectory nearly straight up. "Kubu," she shouted over her shoulder, over the rush of air still audible through the too-thin hull. "If we die, this is Esper's fault."

"Esper's nice," Kubu scolded her. "She helped rescue Kubu. Kubu didn't like it at Not-Mommy's house. Why are we not in the flying house?"

"Kubu," Esper said. "I'm going to try something that isn't easy. I'm going to need quiet. Can you be quiet for a few minutes?"

"Kubu can be quiet," Kubu said. He opened his mouth and snapped it shut.

"Good boy."

Esper was right; he was a good boy. And a big one. As much trouble as they were in to get him back to the *Mobius*, someday soon he wasn't going to fit aboard. First he'd be relegated to the cargo hold for not fitting through doors, then they'd reach a point where they couldn't keep enough food aboard to sate his volcanic appetite.

But that was a problem for another time. For now, they had the next few minutes to live through and perhaps the next twenty or so years in prison.

"We there yet?" Esper asked.

"Watch out through the floor," Tanny snapped. "No, we're not orbital yet."

"My knees go weak looking through the floor," Esper replied. "Like the glass is going to break and—"

"Shut up!" Tanny ordered. "If Mort's taught me anything about wizards, it's that believing is seeing. You might wreck the floor thinking it's fragile."

"Good point."

Esper managed to keep her wits for long enough for the tourist ship to escape Nythy's atmosphere. She brought it to a halt, with the thrusters canceling out the planet's gravity, and opened the comm. "Pursuing vessel, this is... this is the Convocation-controlled vessel *Merlin IX*." Good Lord, she was starting to sound like Carl. "I demand to speak with your ship's wizard."

That ought to have bought them some time.

"*Unregistered vessel, cut engines and prepare to be brought aboard.*" Apparently whoever was after them wasn't taking the bait. How did Carl always manage to find the gullible ones?

"Pursuing vessel, halt or we will be forced to incinerate our hostage," Tanny said into the comm. There was a concerned whine from the passenger compartment. Closing the comm,

Tanny turned and shouted back. "Don't worry, Kubu. It's a trick to help us escape."

Whatever the response from the hostile vessel might have been stopped mattering a moment later. The Black Ocean faded to gray; its stars vanished into the muddy uniformity of astral space. The ship's lights and consoles went dead for a few seconds, then slowly came on again, one by one.

"You did it!" Tanny shouted.

Esper sighed and collapsed into one of the passenger seats. "Looks that way. How far did I drop us?"

"No idea," Tanny replied. "This thing isn't built for astral travel. It doesn't have a depth gauge. So there's... no way to navigate. Or did Mort teach you a trick for that, too?"

"Now we wait," Esper said. "And hope Mort finds Carl and comes after us."

Tanny sighed. "Well, I've heard worse plans. This thing got a holo-projector?"

It was ten hours later. Ten long, tense hours spent discussing life, plans for the future, and contingencies for what they might have to do if help didn't come. But as Tanny was napping with her head pillowed on a snoring Kubu's flank, a voice came over the comm.

"Hello, tiny tin can at a weird astral depth," Carl's voice *came through the tourist ship's comm. "I'm looking for a lost dog. Have you seen him?"*

"Kubu is *not* a dog," Kubu said, lifting his head.

Tanny scrambled for the cockpit.

"Tiny tin can... I don't know what you girls are up to over there but—"

Tanny hit the comm. "Carl! Thank fucking God. I never thought I'd be so happy to hear that reedy voice of yours."

There was a long pause. "No one over here with a reedy voice named Carl. Sorry, you must be the wrong tiny tin can lost at 7.83 astral depth. We'll just keep looking."

"Dammit, Carl," Tanny said. "You can't take gratitude, can you? Just get us on board. We're starving... especially Kubu."

"Roger that, slightly grateful tiny tin can with a snide pilot. Roddy's got your measurements, and Rhiannon's reparking the Camero so you'll fit. Oh, and we're jettisoning that barge of yours before we leave. We don't have room for that shit. What are we, a warehouse?"

"Thanks," Tanny said, slumping into the pilot's seat. "Any idea what was after us?"

"Fuck no," Carl replied. "Mort had us drop to pretty much this exact depth before we got near the system. Had us limp along at the shallow end up 'til then. It's like he knew you'd be right here."

"There's a story there, I think," Tanny said to Esper with the comm closed.

"A couple at least," Esper agreed. "What the hell's a Camero?"

Carl strode into the common room, where three hungry refugees were chowing down on all the food they could shovel into their mouths. In one instance, that amount was frightening.

"Well, I set us a course for border space. No place in particular," Carl announced. "We can sell off the Squall and live off the profits for a long time. I don't think we're going to be welcome in ARGO space for a while."

"Yeah, thanks," Rhiannon griped from the couch, where she sat with Lloyd.

"Where's Mriy?" Esper asked through a mouthful of sandwich. "I haven't seen her since we got back."

"Sleeping off a bullet wound," Mort replied. "Might accept a bit of your help once she's up. Wouldn't let me do more than cauterize the hole."

Carl shuddered. "Yeah, not sure I'd let you do *that* much."

"So where *are* we going?" Tanny asked. "We don't have supplies to be down in the astral forever."

Carl looked to Rhiannon and Lloyd. "Well, we should probably find a place to drop you kids. You didn't sign up for this—"

"For real," Rhiannon muttered.

"But we can make a stop anywhere you want to get off."

Lloyd hugged Rhiannon close. "Thanks. But for now, I think we're fine right here."

EMAIL INSIDERS

You made it to the end! Maybe you're just persistent, but hopefully that means you enjoyed the book. But this is just the end of one story. If you'd like reading my books, there are always more on the way!

Perks of being an Email Insider include:

- Notification of book releases (often with discounts)
- Inside track on beta reading
- Advance review copies (ARCs)
- Access to Inside Exclusive bonus extras and giveaways
- Best of my blog about fantasy, science fiction, and the art of worldbuilding

Sign up for the my Email Insiders list at:
jsmorin.com/updates

BOOKS BY J. S. MORIN

Black Ocean

Black Ocean is a fast-paced fantasy space opera series about the small crew of the *Mobius* trying to squeeze out a living. If you love fantasy and sci-fi, and still lament over the cancellation of *Firefly*, *Black Ocean* is the series for you!

Read about the *Black Ocean* series and discover where to buy at: blackoceanmissions.com

Black Ocean: Astral Prime

Co-written with author M.A. Larkin, *Black Ocean: Astral Prime* hearkens back to location-based space sci-fi classics like *Babylon 5* and *Star Trek: Deep Space Nine*. *Astral Prime* builds on the rich *Black Ocean* universe, introducing a colorful cast of characters for new and returning readers alike. Come along for the ride as a minor outpost in the middle of nowhere becomes a key point of interstellar conflict.

Read about the *Black Ocean: Astral Prime* series and discover where to buy at: astralprimemissions.com

Black Ocean: Mercy for Hire

Black Ocean: Mercy for Hire follows the exploits of a pair of do-gooder bounty hunters who care more about saving the day than securing a payday. The series builds on the rich *Black Ocean* universe, centering on a couple of fan-favorites and introducing a colorful cast for new and returning readers alike. Fans of vigilante justice and heroes who exemplify the word will love this series.

Read about *Black Ocean: Mercy for Hire* and discover where to buy at: mercyforhiremissions.com

Twinborn Chronicles: Awakening

Experience the journey of mundane scribe Kyrus Hinterdale who discovers what it means to be Twinborn—and the dangers of getting caught using magic in a world that thinks it exists only in children's stories.

Twinborn Chronicles: War of 3 Worlds

Then continue on into the world of Korr, where the Mad Tinker and his daughter try to save the humans from the oppressive race of Kuduks. When their war spills over into both Tellurak and Veydrus, what alliances will they need to forge to make sure the right side wins?

Read about the *Mad Tinker Chronicles* and discover where to buy at: twinbornchronicles.com

Robot Geneticists

Robot Geneticists brings genetic engineering into a post-apocalyptic Earth, 1000 years aliens obliterated all life.

These days, even the humans are built by robots.

Charlie7 is the oldest robot alive. He's seen everything from the fall of mankind at the hands of alien invaders to the rebuilding of a living world from the algae up. But what he hasn't seen in over a thousand years is a healthy, intelligent human. When Eve stumbles into his life, the old robot finally has something worth coming out of retirement for: someone to protect.

Read about all of the *Robot Geneticists* books and discover where to buy at: robotgeneticists.com

Sins of Angels

Co-written with author M.A. Larkin, *Sins of Angels* is an epic space opera series set 3000 years after the fall of Earth. With the scope of *Dune* and the adventurous spirit of *Indiana Jones*, it delivers a conflict that spans galaxies and rests on the spirit of brave researcher Professor Rachel Jordan. Follow the complete saga, and watch as the fate of our species hangs in the balance.

Read about *Sins of Angels* and discover where to buy at: sinsofangelsbooks.com

Shadowblood Heir

Shadowblood Heir explores what would happen if the writer of your favorite epic fantasy TV show died before the show ended—and the show was responsible. If you wonder what it would be like if an epic fantasy world invaded our world, this urban fantasy story might give you that glimpse.

Read about *Shadowblood Heir* and discover where to buy at: shadowbloodheir.com

ABOUT THE AUTHOR

I am a creator of worlds and a destroyer of words. As a fantasy writer, my works range from traditional epics to futuristic fantasy with starships. I have worked as an unpaid Little League pitcher, a cashier, a student library aide, a factory grunt, a cubicle drone, and an engineer—there is some overlap in the last two.

Through it all, though, I was always a storyteller. Eventually I started writing books based on the stray stories in my head, and people kept telling me to write more of them. Now, that's all I do for a living.

I enjoy strategy, worldbuilding, and the fantasy author's privilege to make up words. I am a gamer, a joker, and a thinker of sideways thoughts. But I don't dance, can't sing, and my best artistic efforts fall short of your average notebook doodle. When you read my books, you are seeing me at my best.

My ultimate goal is to be both clever and right at the same time. I have it on good authority that I have yet to achieve it.

Connect with me online
jsmorin.com

facebook.com/jsmorinauthor

twitter.com/jsmorinauthor

Made in the USA
Coppell, TX
03 March 2023

13703822R00100